The Flitl

and

The Herring Girls

The Flither Pickers
and
The Herring Girls

*Best wishes
Theresa
Tomlinson*

THERESA TOMLINSON

THE FLITHER PICKERS was first published 1987 by the Littlewood Press

Republished 1992 by Walker Books Ltd 87 Vauxhall Walk, London
SEll 5HJ

Reprinted in 1992

Reprinted in 2005 as part of a compendium edition under the title *Against the Tide* by Random House Children's Books

THE HERRING GIRLS was first published by Julia MacRae 1994 as a Red Fox Book, Random House Children's Books.

Both stories were reprinted in 2005 as part of a compendium volume by Corgi under the title *AGAINST THE TIDE*

© Theresa Tomlinson, 2017

Published by The Old Print Workshop

A CIP catalogue record for this book is available from the British Library.

ISBN 978-0-9955832-0-7

Book layout and design by Clare Brayshaw

Prepared and printed by:

York Publishing Services Ltd
64 Hallfield Road
Layerthorpe
York YO31 7ZQ

Tel: 01904 431213

Website: www.yps-publishing.co.uk

Dedicated to the fishing families of the north-east coast

The inspiration for both the stories came from the photographs of Frank Meadow Sutcliffe, on whom the character of the Picture Man is based and whose expressive black and white photographs illustrate this book. Theresa Tomlinson drew on certain historical facts, such as the launching by the village women of the Runswick Bay lifeboat in 1901, along with her own childhood experiences growing up on the north-east coast and the stories her grandmother related about the fisherwomen who travelled by train from the fishing villages, carrying baskets of fish to sell in the towns. 'The fisherwomen were spotlessly clean and the fish they sold was the best and the freshest you could get.'

The author would like to thank Michael Shaw of THE SUTCLIFFE GALLERY, Flowergate, Whitby for his kind help, advice and support with the Sutcliffe photographs that illustrate this book.

The Flither Pickers

Liza's Story

CHAPTER ONE

I bent my head down and pushed slowly forward into the wind, high on Caedmon's Cliff. Down below I could see Mam and the other flither pickers, out on Sneaton scaur.

I waved and she looked up at us. I dragged my hand back sharp. I shouldn't have made her see us. She'd be mad with me for bringing our Billy out, so early and in such a high wind.

Mam ran towards us, then stopped. I could see her face gone white. Something wrong.

"Liza Welford. Get our Billy back!"

That was my sister Irene shouting at me. She'd come up behind Mam. I'd forgotten Billy as I waved and now I turned to see him balancing on the curved cliff edge that crumbles a bit each day, with a steep drop down to the rocks.

"Billy," I yelled. He flinched as I caught his hand and dragged him back.

"You devil," I screamed and clouted him over the ear. "You've scared our mam."

He started to howl and pull away but I kept tight hold of him, while I turned to look back down below.

I saw that the women had gathered round a hunched figure; that was Mam. Irene pushed them aside, making a way through. At last Mam got up, her face still white. She kept looking up at us.

"Get him back home, you silly lass," Irene shouted.

Mam picked up her bucket and went back to work, searching out the best limpets.

I pulled our sobbing Billy along, down the steps, over the causeway, up to the staithe and back to our cottage.

"I'll be for it 'cause of you," I said. I kept pinching his hand, I was so angry. I pushed him through our doorway, clapping my hand over his mouth.

"Now shut your noise. We mustn't wake Gran, or we'll have Grandpa Welford fretting again."

He looked up at me, silent now, his shoulders shuddering. I took my hand away and pushed my fingers through his curls, fair and soft, like I wished mine were. It was myself I was mad with, not him. I should have taken better care. 'Specially with the family so feared, and Grandma Esther lying in bed sick.

I heard Grandpa Welford's stumping footsteps on the stairs.

"Is that you, our Liza? Fetch a cup of water, will you? Your grandma's wanting to drink."

I took Grandma's favourite blue-flowered china cup from the dresser and carried it out to the pump beyond our yard. Welford's Yard, it's called. My family had lived there for so many years that the cottages that sprang up around had taken our name too.

I jumped as the water splashed over the edge and wasted into the ground. Grandma would have scolded for that.

"Never take it for granted," she'd say. "Good clean spring water we've got. Never waste it. Better water than in any yard in Sandwick Bay."

I carried the cup back inside. A hard, cold lump stuck in my throat; it was thinking of my gran that brought that lump. Her fast tongue, her fierce blue eyes, the way she picked up what you were thinking before you'd spoken. Now she lay abed, getting weaker every day.

Old Miriam, the herb woman, had been called first. She'd given Gran potions, but shaken her head. Then Grandpa

Welford and Daniel, my dad, had talked together and sent for the new doctor from Whitby. That cost; we all knew it must be bad.

The doctor left a bottle of pills and fresh hope, but Grandma got worse. Old Miriam came often now. She brought her potions, but she still shook her head.

"For the pain," she said.

We knew what Miriam meant: 'for the pain, not for the cure'.

I carried the water upstairs and Grandpa opened the door at the top.

"Give your gran a drink, child."

His voice was gruff … he hadn't called me 'child' for a year or so, but then he patted my shoulder and stumped stiff-legged downstairs.

I thought she was asleep, so still she lay, her head propped on two pillows. I went to the stool beside the bed, as quiet as I could, but she caught my movement and her eyelids flickered. I raised her head and helped her drink. Only a sip she managed, and then lay back.

"Thanks Liza, that's better … best water in Sandwick Bay that is … never waste it, my lass."

I'd have sworn she knew I'd just splashed it all over our yard.

"Sit awhile," she begged.

I didn't need asking twice, for I'd rather sit with Gran than be minding our Billy, or being sent off for driftwood, or going to school.

"You should be at school, child," she said.

I shook my head. "I'll not be going today."

"Your mother'll be vexed."

"Nay, she's not bothered these last weeks. She's been glad to have me at home to mind our Billy. Oh but…" I could

3

have bitten my tongue off, for it was Grandma's sickness that had brought that need. It'd been she and Grandpa who'd usually kept an eye on Billy till the last week or two.

"Nay lass, don't look so grim. I know why your mam lets you be home now, but it'll not be for long. I'll soon be gone and your grandpa'll look after Billy again."

I couldn't bear to think how it'd be without her.

"Don't," I whispered. "There's only you that I can tell all to."

"Aye, and that's not right. You should take more notice of your mam, you should."

I nodded my head and thought how many times Gran had said that to me. "Take notice of your mam," she'd say. "She's a good woman, better than you know."

But it was my gran I'd clung to. Gran had looked after me right from being small, while Mam'd been working all day at the bait-gathering, and fixing the lines, and then selling the fish. Gran was warm and lively, quick with a kiss, quick with a slap, but always a tale to tell, while Mam was a quiet, distant sort of woman.

"She were clever," said Gran, catching hold of my hand to make me take notice. "Could have been clever if she'd had the chance, but there weren't these board schools then, and she married our Dan … so young."

"But I'm not like her," I said.

"Your teacher says you're clever. She's taken a lot of trouble with you, has Miss Hindmarch."

"But I'm not wanting schooling. I want to be going with Mam, down on the scaur, doing the work, fetching bait for my dad's lines. Our Irene goes; why not me?"

"No choice." Gran shook her head. "Irene had no choice. Your mam was so weak after Billy. Someone had to fetch the bait and fix the lines. Your dad still had to go with the tide."

"I know," I said. "I know." I'd heard it all often enough, how it was different for me. Because my brother had gone off to fight in that foreign war, they didn't need me for the flither picking. That meant that I could go to school, get some learning, maybe become a pupil teacher if I worked real hard.

Gran coughed and drew a painful shuddering breath, then settled again. "You're lucky to have the choice, my lass," she said.

I nodded and sat there silent, gritting my teeth against the tears.

I heard my name called and a commotion down below. The flither pickers were back.

Gran had fallen asleep, looking exhausted. I hated myself; I'd made her talk too much. I crept from the room and went downstairs to try to keep our Billy happy and out of the way, rolling his marbles in the corner of the yard.

Irene was there, getting herself ready to start to shell the limpets, or flithers as we call them. Mam would get back later for she always walked the long way round, over the bridge, never crossing the causeway with the others.

Irene glowered at me. Now I'd get it.

"You know nowt, our Liza. Don't you ever take Billy up on them cliffs again."

"I caught him back," I said. "I never let him go so near the edge that I couldn't catch him back."

I thought she was going to hit me, so fierce and white she went, but Mam walked into the yard and stared at us.

"What's up?"

Irene shook her head. "Nowt … but I've caught my thumb again."

Mam sat down beside her and I watched as they worked. They shelled the limpets and mussels, caving and skaning, as we call it. They put them to soak and swell in buckets of cold water while they cleaned the lines, picking off the little bits of old bait. Then they set about fixing the fresh shellfish to the sharp hooks, hundreds of hooks to each line, coiling each line carefully in its special basket, or skep, as they worked. An hour it took to bait each line. Strong hands they both had, flicking fast, but scarred hands ... Irene's worse than Mam's. I remembered what my gran had said: how I was lucky to have the choice of schooling or baiting work.

When they'd finished Mam went off to the bakehouse, taking the dough that had been rising by the fire with her. Irene took up her knitting, giving me angry looks. She seemed full of sharp looks and sharp words of late, not like herself at all. I supposed she was upset about Grandma, as we all were in our own different ways. Suddenly she got to her feet and thrust her knitting at me.

"None of your sloppy stitches now." Then, clutching at her stomach, she ran off to our privy at the back.

I looked at the gansey growing fast from her needles. My dad was always needing new leggings or cap or gansey to keep him from freezing out at sea.

I sat down and tried to do a row or two of knitting, but my fingers were clumsy beside Irene's. Still, it was something I had to learn – our own Sandwick stitches, with the waves and herring-bone pattern, though even this skill had a nasty side to it, for if my dad should be drowned and his body washed far away, at least with our special repeat on his gansey they'd know he was a Sandwick man.

CHAPTER TWO

The tide turned late that afternoon. Dad had been to look at the sea and he'd given my mam the nod. That meant they were off.

Billy and me went down to the beach with Mam and Irene walking in front, both with coiled lines in their skeps and the baskets balanced on their heads. We went to give a hand shoving the coble out, for we have no other way to launch our boats in Sandwick Bay. Even our heavy lifeboat, the *Francis Welford,* has to be dragged over the sand and hauled right out into the sea.

Aunt Hannah Welford and Mary our cousin were there and we all helped push out my dad and Uncle Jack in our sturdy coble, the *Sneaton Lass.* John Ruswarp was going off in the *Lily Belle* with his younger brother Sam and Mrs Ruswarp was there to help them shove.

Their dad had been drowned five years back and John had taken over his father's boat though he was only fifteen at the time. My dad had helped him learn the work. There'd been three great lads all of an age, all learning together. There was John Ruswarp, our Frank and my cousin Ned Welford. Always laughing and teasing they were. They'd carry me on their shoulders and bring me liquorice back from Whitby … now there was only John Ruswarp still in Sandwick Bay.

They'd gone out together one night, all three, though my dad had warned that the sea was too lumpy. There'd been a storm and my cousin Ned was drowned. Our Frank changed after that; he seemed feared of going out himself. He said it was getting so that the fishing was not worthwhile, what with the new-fangled trawlers draining the sea of the fry.

Then the war in South Africa had come and there'd been a call for volunteers. Our Frank went off to Scarborough and joined the Green Howards. My dad was broken-hearted about it.

"If he thinks it's hard working the boats, he'll find it harder where he's going," he said. Dad never mentioned Frank's name these days, but he picked up all the news he could from South Africa, and lately John Ruswarp had talked about following our Frank and joining up.

John was twenty and a handsome-looking fellow, but that day Irene didn't run over to him as she usually did. She didn't even seem to look his way and it was fat Nelly Wright that was hanging round John's boat, casting spiteful looks our way and talking at the top of her voice.

We stood on the beach and watched the boats out, then turned back to the village. Mam and Hannah walked up the beach together. Irene and Mary, who were the same age, followed close behind, heads bent together, whispering. They left me out, as though I were a child, left me with Billy tagging at my wet skirts. Mrs Ruswarp came puffing up behind me.

"Here's your pal, she'll be looking for you," she said, pointing up at the staithe.

It was her daughter Mary Jane that she pointed too, waving and hallooing, fresh from school and I was glad to see her.

"Now then Liza, not at school again?" She scrambled over the shingle and took my arm.

I shook my head. "Y'see I'm not, daft ha'p'orth."

"Is your gran real bad then?"

I nodded and we walked on together arm in arm.

"Miss Hindmarch was asking after you today, saying that it were a pity if you fell behind."

I shrugged my shoulders. I couldn't care less if I never went to school again.

"I heard tell," said Mary Jane, "that some of the younger lads at Whitby were wagging off school and the kid-catcher chased them all the way down to the harbour. So they stripped off their clothes and ran straight into the water."

"They never did."

"Stripped naked they did and the kid-catcher, he was furious, but you can be sure he wasn't for getting himself wet. He left them there and turned back into town, looking for others."

"Well, there's a trick," I said.

"Yes, but I've not told you all. Those lads hadn't come out of the water before this picture chap who makes photographs comes staggering down to the front with his boxes and his props, and he shouts to them, 'Stay where you are lads and I'll give you a penny."

"A penny to share?"

"No, a penny apiece. He set up his photographing things and made a picture of them – there in the water, stripped naked. A penny apiece he gave them and they say they're down there every day since then, all ready to strip and hoping he'll be back."

"They'd not set kid-catcher on me," I said. "Not this far from Whitby and me a great lass, old enough to be working with me mam."

"No," said Mary Jane. "They'd not bother with a lass, that's true, but Miss Hindmarch, she says a lass as clever as you should be at school. Best pupil she thinks you are, and I wish you'd come back for I can't work my 'rithmetic without you to help me."

I went to sit with Gran when I got back home … just sat there quiet beside her while she slept. Her breathing was faint, I thought it gone, but then she opened her eyes and took my hand.

"Glad you're here," she said. "Something … must tell."

I bent close for her voice was weak now.

"William," she said.

"William? You mean our Billy?"

She shook her head and tried again. "William Archer."

I'd not heard of William Archer, but Archer was a name I knew well enough. It was Mam's name before she was married.

"She called … she called Billy after him."

"Don't talk now Gran. Rest."

"No," she said, all agitated. "Must tell. I was there, I saw her. She's feared … more than you know, your mam."

Her breath came difficult. I lifted the cup to her lips and helped her drink. She lay back on the pillows, her mouth working soundlessly.

"Rest Gran," I said. "Tell me in the morning and I'll listen well," but she was already asleep, exhausted with her effort.

It was late that night that I was woken from a deep sleep. Mam was shaking me. "Get up lass and fetch Miriam, for your gran is took real bad."

I got up from the mattress that I shared with Irene, knuckling the sleep from my eyes. Mam wrapped my shawl around me and pushed me to the ladder that led down from our loft. I stumbled down our stairs, my heart thudding, and hastened out onto the top staithe and down to Miriam's cottage.

She opened quickly to my knocking. "So it's time," she said. There was no surprise. She picked up her basket and followed me.

Gran died in the early hours. Miriam sent us downstairs while she did the laying out. I sat at our kitchen table and couldn't stop shaking. Irene put her arms around me, hugging me close … my kind big sister once again.

Mam kept calling up the stairs where Grandpa sat. He wouldn't move from the top step, not for all Mam's persuading. He sat up there with his head in his hands and wouldn't come down.

I hated that black bonnet they gave me; it smelt of lavender and death.

"You'll wear it for respect," said Mam.

Black silk it was, made in our special Sandwick way from a yard of silk with five pleats measured across the top and a double frill round the bottom. The frill was supposed to stop the water from the fish baskets dripping on your neck, but nobody would ever carry fish on a black silk bonnet. It was made special, for funerals, and we had plenty of them. I shook it out and tied it beneath my chin, swallowing hard.

"I'll wear it for Gran," I said.

Daniel, my dad, missed the tide for two days. When he returned from the sea and found his mother dead, he sat by the fire and wept.

Mam didn't cry; I don't think she found time for there was so much to do. Irene was quiet, shut off in a world of her own, but she roused herself to go out with me and Mary, bidding our relations and neighbours to come to the funeral. That's always the job of young women in our bay.

Grandpa was the one we worried about most. Such a fine man my grandpa was, real respected in our community. He'd been the lifeboat cox like his father Francis, who our lifeboat's named for. Grandpa has saved so many lives, taking out our heavy boat that's so difficult to launch. Folk still talk about the day that Grandpa went out three times in that dreadful storm that sank the Whitby lifeboat. Our boat survived, though the crew exhausted themselves and one man died of pneumonia. Grandpa's leg was crushed; he's dragged it ever since. My grandpa, who was our hero, wouldn't speak to anyone after Grandma's death. He shrank into himself … shrunk small and grey and lost.

I'd got no tears but I knew they were there, welling up tight inside me. After the funeral Irene walked off with John Ruswarp, who'd been waiting for her outside the church. I was surprised Mam didn't call her back to help with the funeral dinner. So it was me who did most of the helping. I did my best and worked hard to see that all our guests got plenty, for it was part of showing respect for the dead one, giving a good feast after the service. But when the plates were cleared and the talking and drinking began, I slipped away.

I went down to the beach, for I knew I'd have a good cry and I didn't want them to see. I sat on Plosher Rock, as Mary Jane and me call it, after the big five-man cobles that go from Whitby Harbour. I pulled the silk bonnet from my head and held it on my lap as I stared out to sea. The tears came slow and choking at first, then pouring freely, bringing relief. I picked up the bonnet from my lap and set it carefully on the dry rock. I'd be in trouble if I soaked it, for it must be wrapped up with lavender and put away for the next sad day.

It was only as calm came that I thought of the night that Gran had died and remembered with a sudden catch of breath that she'd wished to tell me something … something about young William Archer.

CHAPTER THREE

It was quiet when I got back and I found Irene standing at the table in the corner of the yard, back in her working dress and apron. She saw my red eyes and swollen face.

"You must put it behind you, lass," she said, quite kind. "Go change your dress; there's a line needs mucking. Dad's gone to rest for a while, for he must go with the tide tonight."

I changed my clothes and went to help. Irene was talkative but I could see that she was still upset. Hannah and Mary had brought bait for us early that morning and we'd the worst job to do now, for we'd baited lines that Dad had not been able to use, so the bait had gone foul. Mucking we called it, and a muckier job there never was. We hated mucking but it had to be done. Irene's hands shook as she pulled the scraps of stinking bait from the barbs, working slow for her. I looked from her hands to her face, and she caught that glance. She dropped the line and lifted the backs of her hands to her eyes. Quiet tears ran down her cheeks, tears that she couldn't wipe for her hands were slimed with mouldy bait.

I was shocked. I couldn't think when I'd last seen her cry. "Is it Gran?"

She shook her head. "Not just Gran. You'll know soon enough … so I'll say now. I'm to have a child."

I blinked. I couldn't believe what she was saying.

"Aye, you'll be shocked," she said. "But you don't know yet how strong it can be, that feeling … that feeling when you're sweet on a lad."

I couldn't think what to say and she wiped her hands on her torn apron, searching for a clean corner to dry her eyes.

"Is … is it John Ruswarp?"

"Aye, him. Him who wants to be joining the Army, who wants to be off fighting, so far away."

I pulled myself together then. I remembered how she'd been sick and running to the privy.

"I should have known," I said. "I should have guessed, a great girl like me. I've thought of nothing but Gran."

"Nay, how should you know such things? You're nobbut a bairn and you stay that way, our Liza."

I went and put my arms round her, hugging her tight, frightened for her.

"I fear 'tis the worst to come," she said. "Mam knows and she's to tell Dad."

"What does Mam say?"

"She says I'm a fool, but I'm not the first and she'll take my side. Best get Dad told, she says, even though he's so sad for Gran. Best get our troubles over, though I dread what he'll have to say."

We stood there quiet, but then Irene seemed to brace herself.

"Now then, our Liza, this won't do. We're forgetting the lines. We must get these done or we'll have trouble indeed."

We returned to our work, but it was different. She was working slowly, her hands shaking still, and I worked really hard for once, trying to take the lead. I took the line.

"I'll coil," I said, flicking the baited hooks aside as carefully as I could, thinking that I must learn to do this better. Irene would find it hard in the coming months. They'll need me even more, I thought.

We finished the lines and Mam went upstairs to wake Dad for the tide and we heard him shouting.

"She's told him," said Irene, her eyes filling with tears.

When Mam came down she sent us both out with Billy.

"Away with you," she said. "Take Billy up to the heather for a bit or air. Hannah and Mary'll help get the boats off. He'll feel different in the morning. He likes John Ruswarp more than most."

We walked up the hillside, past the old chapel, Billy running ahead. I felt strange with Irene, as though she were someone I didn't really know. I was scared for her, but pleased that she'd told me so much. Treating me like a woman for once. I couldn't help thinking about her and John Ruswarp, what they must have done … up there on the hillside, I guessed, where all the couples walk in summer. I knew about that — well, some of the girls at school talked about nothing else. I thought it sounded horrible and I told Mary Jane that I wasn't ever going to let any man do that to me.

I kept thinking about Irene having a bairn, too. I'd be real frightened of that; that was another thing they talked about at school. I couldn't forget how Rachel Danby had told how her sister had screamed so loud they'd all been sent out into the yard and they could still hear her screaming from there.

I remembered our Billy being born. It had been a long and difficult birth, but I never heard a scream or any sound from Mam, though I'd been at home all the time. I was sitting on Grandpa's knee, sniffing at his pipe and poking fresh tobacco into it, when Grandma Esther came to tell us that Billy was born.

Even though I was so small I knew that Mam was very poorly for a long time afterwards and Miriam had said that there'd be no more bairns for Mam.

Now it was going to happen to Irene and she didn't seem to be worrying about that part of it. She was just unhappy about what Dad would have to say and John wanting to go off to join the fighting.

She told me that John wanted them to be wed. He'd always wanted that, but he still wished to go off to South Africa like Frank. He wanted to make something of himself … so he said.

We sat down near the bank top where the heather begins, watching Billy jumping and hiding in thick purple clumps. We pulled our shawls tight, for though there was a bright sun, we were well into autumn and a chilly wind blew.

"That Nelly Wright," said Irene. "She'll have something to say when she hears. Such a wag-tongued gossip she is and she's sweet on John herself. She'll be mouthing it all the way to Whitby, she will."

"Nay," I said. "Who cares what fat Nelly says? She'd better not say owt about my sister when I'm there."

Irene smiled and squeezed my hand. "You're a grand sister, our Liza," she said.

Irene had brought her knitting for no time should be wasted and Irene could knit without looking at her hands. She stared out across the bay, her fingers working of their own accord. She was a fine young woman and I could see why John might think her bonny. Even in her working clothes she looked good, with her pink cheeks and clear skin and her hair done in the new fashion that she took such trouble with, curling her fringe in rags each week. She had a little plaited bun at the back and a thick fringe brushed forwards in shiny brown curls, like the new Queen Alexandra. Irene's hair was the same colour as mine. It was only Billy who'd got the fair curls we both wanted.

I asked Irene about William Archer. I told her how Gran had wanted me to know. I wouldn't have asked her before, but she seemed so much more my friend that day.

"Do you know owt of a William Archer?"

"Do you mean that little lad who was Mam's brother?"

16

"Ah, that must be him," I said. "Gran wanted to tell me about him, but it was the night she died. She never got it said and I didn't know what she meant."

"I don't know much about him," said Irene. "Just that he was drowned and Mam was with him and it upset her so much that she'll not cross the causeway. That's why she always goes the long way round."

"Gran was telling me that I should take more notice of Mam. Gran was always telling me that."

"Aye, so you should. There's not every mother would take her daughter's side, like Mam is with me. Aunt Hannah would know about that little lad William, though. Her and Mam have always been close. I dare say Aunt Hannah would have been there at the time."

We were silent for a while, Billy still happily playing in the heather behind us.

"There they go," I said, pointing down to the beach. We couldn't see very clear, but we could tell which was our boat, the *Sneaton Lass*, and could see Mam and Dad, both with skeps on their heads. We saw John Ruswarp go down with his mam and it looked like Mary Jane with them. She'd not been to school because of the funeral.

Dad went over to John, but we couldn't tell what went on. Time passed and they were still together on the beach, though the other cobles were out. Irene's knitting went faster and faster.

"Oh dear," she said. "There's a to-do, I know there is. Would Dad hit him, do you think?"

"Nay," I said. "John's that much bigger than Dad."

Irene laughed and I joined in. We giggled together, but Irene laughed on after I'd stopped … wild laughing, then suddenly it turned into desperate sobbing that frightened me. I put my arms round her and Billy came to stare at us.

I didn't know what to do. I thought of Grandma Esther and missed her bitterly. She'd have known what to say and what to do.

"It's all right," said Irene, pushing me away and smiling wet-faced at Billy. "It's all right, our Billy," she said, pulling him onto her knee while I fished around for the knitting she'd dropped, trying to save the stitches.

We sat on, staring down at the jumbled red roofs of our village. The cottages are crammed tight together on the steep bank side, so that kitchens often overlook their neighbours' bedroom window and we all know each other's business … it can't be helped. We sat silent, watching the smoke puthering out of the chimneys and the washing flapping on the lines.

At last we saw that John had gone off in his boat and Dad and Uncle Jack were following.

"Now then, our Billy," said Irene, "it's time we got you home."

Mam was laying out left-overs from the funeral dinner when we got back.

"Good," she said. "You're here. You can eat up these bits for your suppers. Go wash your hands Billy, then sit up at the table."

I couldn't believe it was only that morning that we'd been in our funeral clothes; so much had happened that day. Irene and I stood silent, not knowing how to put the question.

"Now don't stand there like ninnies. Get set down."

"But Mam," said Irene. "What's been said?"

"It wasn't so much saying as shouting," said Mam, "but that's for the best, I think. It was Mrs Ruswarp I was sorry for, her knowing nowt about it and she was so shamed when she realised. Hannah and I walked back with her, though, and told her all and I think she feels better now. Mary Jane was listening too, her eyes wide and her ears flapping. I've never seen John so eager to be off, shouting at his mother and her not understanding. Their Sam knew what was up all right and I'm glad to see you've told our Liza."

"Aye," Irene said and she reached for my hand.

"Never mind," Mam said. "I think the worst is over. He'll have calmed down, will your dad, by the time he's had a night out there. So get yourselves set down and make the most of a decent meal. Your gran wouldn't like to see it wasted."

CHAPTER FOUR

Dad waited for John on the top staithe when he got back the next morning. Mam had been right. They sat together for a while talking quiet and friendly.

When Dad got back to our cottage, he kissed Irene and hugged her and told her she was a silly lass. He'd talked to Uncle Jack while he was out and thought a lot about Esther, their mam, and he'd come to think that it was fine, that a new life should be coming when one so loved had just gone. He said he'd rather she married John Ruswarp than any other, though she could have waited for chapel first. Still, we'd make the best of it and he'd talk to John about the Army and try to get him to change his mind and stay.

I met Mary Jane down on the beach and we went arm in arm to our special rock. Mary Jane was full of it.

"Well fancy our John and your Irene! Fancy them going and doing that. I couldn't believe my ears when I heard all that shouting going on. Eeeh, your dad was vexed, and the whole village heard about it. Weren't you surprised?"

"Well … our Irene had told me," I said. "So I knew there'd be a to-do."

"I'll like to be the auntie though," said Mary Jane.

"But it's me as will be the auntie."

"Oh …" said Mary Jane, frowning with working it out. "So you will, for Irene's your sister, but John's my brother so I'll be the auntie, too."

"We'll both be aunties," I said. "Both aunties to the same bairn. That makes us like relations, you and me."

We liked the thought of that and we sat there planning the things we'd do. The best aunties in the world we would be.

Along the beach came Nelly Wright and her little gang of friends. Older than us they were and all of them had been bait-gatherers for a year or so. Some of the lasses were kind enough if you saw them by themselves or with their mams, but when they all got together with Nelly Wright as ringleader, a real rough noisy lot they could be.

"I've not seen your Irene today," Nelly shouted. "I hear she's got the belly ache, the belly ache that don't go away."

They all shrieked with laughter and shoved at each other with their elbows.

I jumped down from my rock so angry I'd forgotten to be scared.

"Don't you speak about my sister. She's better than the lot of you."

They fell about laughing again.

"Can you hear the flither squeaking?" yelled Nelly. Then she pointed at Mary Jane who'd come and thrust her arm through mine. "Aye, and look at that saucy face. Saucy like her brother she is. You wouldn't believe the tales I could tell about that lad … though I'm not so low as to let him give me the belly ache."

They slapped each other on the backs, still shaking with their laughing, and turned to walk on up the beach.

I stuck my tongue out at their backs and Mary Jane, she followed behind at a safe distance, holding her skirt out behind her, waving it from side to side, imitating fat Nelly's wobbly walk.

We went back to Plosher Rock, giggling ourselves now. We weren't going to let them spoil us being aunties, whatever they might say.

"I wish our John wouldn't go on about joining the Army though," said Mary Jane. "I can't bear the thought of him going off to the war. He might get himself killed, then the poor bairn'd have no dad."

"Aye," I agreed with her. "I do miss our Frank, though it were grand that day when we went over to Scarborough to wave them off. It was such a to-do. Folk were throwing flowers and bands were playing and everyone was singing and shouting. The lads looked so smart in their uniforms and folk were saying how volunteers had never before gone off like that to fight with the Regulars."

"Our John wishes he'd gone with them," Mary Jane said.

I sighed. "It was so lovely," I said. "But suddenly they were gone and we've heard nowt since, only snippets of news that my dad picks up in Whitby and we don't know whether our Frank's alive or dead. We heard that some of the lads came back last August, but never a word have we heard of Frank."

We sat on our rock quietly thinking about it for a while, but then we turned our heads at what seemed to be a bit of a commotion up in the village. A group of lads came walking down by the staithe following a man, a gentleman almost, but loaded up with boxes and bits and pieces. The lads were carrying things, too. There were folded sticks and an umbrella with black material draped at the sides.

"Well I never," said Mary Jane. "I do believe it's him."

"Whatever do you mean?"

"It's him … the picture man, the one I told you about."

"Oooh … are you sure it's him?"

"Who else could it be?"

We watched as they walked along the staithe to Old Miriam's cottage. We couldn't hear what was going on, but it was clear enough. He wished to make a picture of Miriam. We could tell how pleased she was, flustered and smiling and brushing down her skirt. It took a long time to get the camera fixed, but the picture man had the lads all quiet and good and running at his beck and call.

Miriam sat up straight and smart, like the squire's lady herself, but the picture man didn't seem to be in any hurry to get his photograph done. He talked on and on to Miriam, and we'd got a fine view of it all up on our rock. At last, when Miriam picked up her knitting and leaned back in her chair chatting ... suddenly the picture was being made.

We watched them packing everything up ready to leave and we were just going to get down from our rock to follow the procession of lads when the picture man looked our way. He stopped for a moment and held his hand up to shade his eyes, then he started to walk towards us. Our mouths dropped open; straight towards us he came. Mary Jane looked behind to see if there was someone else ... but there was no one. We looked at each other scared for there was no doubt but he was coming over to us. I was that shocked it fair took my breath away, but there he was standing before our rock, bowing slightly and lifting his hat, the gang of lads waiting farther back.

"You make a fine picture up there on the rock, young ladies. I'd be pleased to make a picture of you."

We stared, then Mary Jane giggled and I couldn't help it; I was giggling too, looking back at this slim man, quite tall with a kind smile and fine bushy beard.

"Do I have your permission, young ladies?"

We giggled again and nodded. "Can if you like."

Again he took a long time setting his camera up. He talked to us as he worked, asking our names and did we live in the bay.

He set up three spindly legs, fastened together, then fixed his camera box on top. A bit wobbly it looked, balanced on the shingle, and he had the lads looking round for a flat-topped stone to fix beneath the back leg. At last it was fixed, but then he had to move the whole contraption farther back

and find another stone. At last he seemed satisfied and stayed beneath the cape saying, "That's good … that's good."

He had to bend his long legs to get himself to the right height.

"You can't see much in there, can you?" asked Mary Jane, grown bold.

"I can see you fine young ladies," he said. "I see you fine, but upside-down."

We both laughed at that and the laughing made me cheeky. I leant right over, propping up my head with my hand. "Why should we not sit like this then?"

"You goose," said Mary Jane.

"Stay just like that," came the picture man's voice.

So bursting with sauciness, but frozen still, we had our picture made.

"That's done," he said, appearing from under the cape.

"But that was daft," I said.

"Aye, a bit of fun, but I think a good picture. I'll send a copy for your mothers if you tell me where you live."

We did more than tell him, we walked back up the beach with him and showed him our cottages. He spoke all polite to Mam, treating her like a lady. Mam was all shamed with her apron dirty from the skaning and her hands all slimed.

We walked up the hill with him, helping to carry his boxes … up to the pony and trap waiting at the top. He asked us if we went to school and Mary Jane told him how Miss Hindmarch wished me back there.

"Is that Miss Cicely Hindmarch?" he asked.

"Yes," said Mary Jane.

"I'm acquainted with Miss Hindmarch," he said. "A good teacher and a clever woman. If Miss Hindmarch thinks well of you, you must be an able pupil."

Mary Jane nudged me hard.

"Perhaps you should return to school," he said.

"Nay, book learning's got nowt to do with the likes of me."

He looked thoughtful for a moment and I thought that perhaps I'd sounded rude, but he smiled and lifted his hat. He loaded up the trap with his boxes and went on his way.

"He never gave us any pennies," said Mary Jane.

CHAPTER FIVE

Mam was packing a parcel of fish-heads wrapped in cloth when I got back.

"When you've finished with having your head turned, you can run an errand for me. Take these over to poor Annie Lythe. Tell her I'm sorry it's only the heads."

Poor Annie Lythe, as everyone called her, had lost her husband: drowned at sea, the familiar way. Annie had six children all of them younger than me and we knew she was having a struggle to raise them, but she managed to keep them out of the workhouse somehow. She took in washing and we all gave what we could to help. It wasn't like charity; it was just 'the right thing to do', for we all knew that the next family orphaned might be ours. Mam usually sent a decent fish. If it was fish-heads for Annie Lythe, then it would be fish-head stew for us too. With the bad weather starting, Dad'd not be able to get out every time and we'd be mucking the lines again.

Annie's cottage was next to Aunt Hannah's and I saw Hannah and Mary sat out at the back, baiting lines as I passed. I remembered how Irene had said that Aunt Hannah was the one to ask if I wanted to know more about William Archer, Mam's young brother. But Aunt Hannah has a bit of a sharp tongue and I hurried past them and on to Annie's.

To find Annie Lythe, you had to fight your way through sheets and petticoats and frilly drawers all hanging from lines across the yard. She was turning the poss stick in her dolly tub, her sleeves rolled high and her muscles straining, her small kitchen filled with steam. Her oldest daughter lanky Dory was helping her turn the stick, her hair plastered to her wet forehead. We call her lanky Dory as she's so tall, but I like her well enough.

"Now then Dory," I said.

She stopped her work and smiled, quickly wiping her hands on a rag.

"Is that for us?" she asked, reaching for the parcel that I carried.

"Aye, o' course it is," I told her.

"Thank your mam kindly," Annie said.

"'Fraid it's only fish-heads," I told her.

"I know the catches have been small so it's most kind of her," insisted Annie.

Her two youngest girls came then to stand before me, tugging at my skirt.

"Nay, I've got no liquorice today," I said, wishing that I'd saved a bit when Dad brought some back from Whitby with him last week. Their dresses were clean but worn and holed. Annie had little time to spare from her laundry work to see to her own girls' clothes.

"I heard about your Irene's trouble," said Annie speaking quietly. "Tell her that I wish her well, will you? When you know how easy life is lost, you value a new life coming."

I thanked her and said goodbye. It's funny, I thought. Funny how it's often those that has least that manages to be kindest.

I dawdled a little by Aunt Hannah's door, wanting to speak to her, but I needed to gather my courage for Aunt Hannah won't suffer fools. She's not quiet like our mam; she always has plenty to say.

"Well, Liza," said Hannah when she spied me, "you're here at the right time. Get yourself sat down and coil this line, for Mary's to go to Walter Snaith's to fetch our new skeps. You'll earn yourself a cup of tea if you do that."

At least you didn't need an invitation with Hannah.

I sat and helped, but couldn't think how to ask what I wanted, till Hannah herself showed me the way.

"You should be getting back to school, Liza," she said. "That'd please your mam, now that poor Esther's gone."

"Why ... I would," I said, "but with Grandpa taken to his bed, there's none of them left to look after Billy but me."

"Aye, there's some as would take Billy down on the beach with them to let him play while the picking's done, but not Martha."

"Grandma Esther wanted me to know something about that," I said, grabbing at my chance.

"Whatever do you mean? Speak sense, lass. What did Esther want you to know?"

I swallowed hard and tried again. "Esther wanted to tell me about young William Archer, but it was the night she died and she never got it said."

"Aah," said Hannah, quite soft for her. "Esther wanted to tell you that, did she? That's what you're here for then. Well, Esther did usually know what's best and I think we should respect her wishes."

I nodded, uncomfortable, while Hannah inspected me.

"I'm not sure as you shouldn't ask your mam ... but maybe it's easier for someone else to say. I'll tell you what I can."

"I know that William Archer was Mam's young brother," I said. "And I know he was drowned, but then we've all had family drowned haven't we, like ..."

"Aye, like our Ned. True enough, but it's usually in bad weather or a storm and you dread it, but you half expect it. William Archer, he was drowned on a sunny spring afternoon, the sea had seemed as calm as you could wish. We were nearby, but we never saw owt amiss ... not till it was too late."

"You were there then, Aunt Hannah?"

"Oh aye, I was there." Her face went sad and she spoke so quiet I could hardly believe it was my aunt.

"There was me, Esther and old Mrs Lythe – that's Annie's mother-in-law. There was your mam's mother Katherine Archer, too, and we were all fetching the flithers. I'd just started to help with it and I felt jealous of Martha, your mam, her being that bit younger than me and her still being treated like a child. She was left to splash about near the causeway with little William. She'd been told to take care of him, mind."

It felt strange to think of my mam being a young lass and having to look after her young brother, like I did Billy.

"It was Esther who saw it first," said Hannah. "'What's up with your Martha?' she said. Katherine looked … well we all looked and there she was lying face-down near the causeway, close to the water's edge and the tide going out, for we'd not been picking long. She wasn't shouting or making any sound, but she was kicking and punching at the sand."

I shuddered when I heard that. I couldn't imagine my mam behaving so odd.

"'She's lost that lad,' said Katherine. 'She's let him run off up the staithe.' We wandered over to her. We weren't in any hurry, but when we got close we saw that she was in a right state, slavering and biting at the sand. Katherine went and pulled her to her feet. 'Where's the lad?' she asked. 'Has he run off?' Martha didn't answer, just kept opening and shutting her mouth, but she pointed to the sea. Well, then we did worry. Katherine slapped your mam hard across the face. 'Where's the lad?' she asked again and at last poor Martha spoke. 'In the sea.'"

I'd stopped my work on Mary's line and Aunt Hannah never even noticed, so tense her face had gone.

"We stared out to sea," she said, "but there was nowt and it looked so calm we couldn't believe that the lad was in there. Katherine, she suddenly made up her mind to take no chances. She put down her swill of flithers and walked straight into the sea – clothes, boots and all – and once she'd done it we all seemed to think that she was right. We followed her and we looked and looked. We went out as deep as we dared, but we found nothing. Even then we weren't sure. We made Katherine come back in. We told her not to worry, we said he'd come running down the staithe before long. We stopped our picking; the men'd have to stay at home that night, for a young lad's life means more than a good catch.

"We took Katherine home and searched the village. Martha was forgotten. Where she went, I don't know, but it was Miriam who brought her home that night. Nobody held her to blame – it was the sea – but I think she blamed herself and as far as I know your mam has never crossed the causeway since."

"But how had William gone?"

"We've never really known, but drowned he was and his body washed up at Sandsend. We could only think that he must have been caught in one of those strong currents. You can never trust the sea … it takes those it wants."

I sat frozen, staring at my aunt, trying to take in all she'd said. Seeing my mam as a child and her so frightened and distraught that she'd near gone mad.

"Esther was right," said Hannah, more her usual self. "It's best that you know. Don't mock your mam when she goes traipsing over the bridge or fussing over Billy, and think how she manages to get herself down on that beach, working all the time to feed you bairns."

I nodded. I was chilled right through and I needed Hannah's hot sweet tea to warm me again, but Hannah wasn't one to let you sit and stew.

"Seeing as you're here and Mary's not back, you can come down to the beach with me and your Uncle Frank. Take that wreath from Mary's peg and get that skep fixed on your head."

My aunt went inside for Uncle Frank and I reached the padded band down and pulled it round my head. I lifted the skep I'd been working on and got it comfortably settled in its place. I was glad to be having a job to do, after what I'd heard, and at least Aunt Hannah treated me like I was useful.

CHAPTER SIX

As the weeks went by and the sun shone lower in the sky, the winds blew cold and our lives settled into the hard pattern that each winter brings. The men had to use the longer lines and go farther out. That meant more bait to be fetched and the weather worse for doing it.

Mam and Hannah made some visits up the Cleveland coast to sell fish to the steelworkers' families. They had done this before, keeping back as much fish as they could carry from the dealer who waited above the staithe with his donkey carts. It was a real tramp for them, carrying the fish baskets on their heads padded with wreaths, but they could make a bit of extra money that way, before the worst weather set in. They were getting the reputation of being sharp business women.

The flither pickers began to talk of a trek. This was something they often had to do during the winter months, but now they thought it best to get it done whilst it was still autumn, before the worst weather came.

There was such a great amount of flither picking and mussel picking done in our bay that the shellfish would become few, and small at that. So the women would organise a trek. They'd set off with a great load of sacks and swills and walk away down the coast in search of a right good supply. They had to go past Whitby, ignoring the limpets there, for they were needed by the Whitby pickers and a large supply they needed too. So our Sandwick women had to go to the scaur way past Whitby and a good fifteen miles that was. It was all a bit of a fuss and a palaver; they had to find relations or friends to stay overnight with in Whitby.

We'd send the donkey carts over the cliffs to carry the flithers back. Then the women would be up early the next morning and walking back to get the caving and skaning done, so's not to lose another day's fishing.

"Can't I come with you this time?" I begged Mam, when she and Hannah were making their plans.

"Nay," said Mam. "A trek's no jolly outing and you'll stay to see to Billy and your grandpa … though I wish you might be back in school once your grandpa is himself again."

I sighed and then began to make more arguments, but I caught Aunt Hannah looking at me, so I shut my mouth and went out onto the staithe.

I didn't want to be getting back to school at all, but I hated Grandpa being sick. Mam talked to Hannah about it and I could tell she was worried. The thing was that you couldn't really say what was wrong with him. He lay in bed all day and refused to eat most of the food that we carried up to him. Even Billy couldn't rouse him. Miriam said there was nothing to be done. She said that he was suffering from grief and that had to run its course. We should leave him be, she said, and he'd come back to us in his own good time. But the weeks went by and he kept to his bed.

I sat out there on the top staithe, remembering how happy I'd been when I was a little girl. Grandma Esther would wrap me up warm in my bonnet and shawl and I'd go out with Grandpa in all but the worst of weather and we'd sit up there on the top staithe. We never sat alone, for every person passing would stop to speak. Sometimes we'd be surrounded by a great gang of children, all of them there to listen to Grandpa's stories. I was so proud to be sat on Grandpa's knee, so proud to be his grandchild. He'd tell stories of shipwrecks, of smuggling, of our lifeboats and the different coxswains, the rescues that he'd made himself, but my favourite story came from a time way back: the story of Simon Wise.

Grandpa would tell how a mysterious stranger had come from the forests over Pickering way and his name, so he said, was Simon Wise. He'd taken to fishing and had gone out one night with an old fisherman who'd befriended him. That night they'd been attacked by a French ship, a man-o'-war. Simon Wise had told his friend not to be afraid and he'd taken up his bow and arrow and shot every Frenchman that tried to board the small boat. The last few members of the crew surrendered and asked Simon Wise aboard. It turned out to be a pirate ship, loaded with stolen gold that the pirates offered him in payment for their lives. Simon sent the pirates on their way, telling them not to pick on small fishing boats again, and he gave away all the gold they'd given him to the poor fisher-folk of the coast. He then returned to the forest he came from and later became known in other parts of the country as the outlaw Robin Hood.

Mam, Dad and Mrs Ruswarp started to make plans for Irene's wedding. It was to be as soon as we could get it arranged, keeping a bit of decency, as Dad said, for the banns to be read in the Chapel at Loftus. So we'd got the date fixed for late November and, although it was to be a bit of a rushed do, my dad insisted that we'd make it a fine wedding and hold our heads high. We'd have all the traditional fun and frills: a reception in the village hall and dancing late into the night, and of course we'd have John Ruswarp's coble hauled up onto the beach to be decorated with flags and bunting and paper flowers. Mam said she wanted to get the trek done first, then we'd have an outing to Whitby to buy the stuff for Irene's dress. Mary Jane and me were to be bridesmaids.

Mam said two were enough in the circumstances, instead of the usual six.

I got up early on the morning of the trek and Billy and me walked along the beach to set them on their way. When we reached Caedmon's Cliff, Mam sent us back.

"And you see you get Billy back safe," she said. "The tide's on the turn so don't dawdle."

I didn't argue as I once might have done. "Yes, Mam," I answered meek enough, and after we'd watched them trudge away beneath the cliffs I took his hand and I did take care, for after what Hannah had told me I could see why Mam had taken fright when I let Billy wander on the cliffs. I'd thought a bit more about our Billy, too. He was a fine little brother really and I wouldn't be without him. We played follow-my-leader as we went back to the village and I let him be the leader. I even enjoyed seeing him so delighted when he made me walk backwards, twice round Plosher Rock and then crawl on all fours over the scaur.

It was quiet in the village for most of the women had gone on the trek, leaving only the young and the old, and the men still resting, having got back from the sea in the early hours. Billy and me sat on the top staithe where Grandpa used to sit.

Old Walter Snaith came and joined us for a while, working away at one of his baskets. Walter made all the baskets we needed for our work: swills for collecting flithers, flatter skeps for the long lines and big fish-baskets, too. He asked after my grandpa and said that it was a sad thing indeed. He'd known Grandpa well; they'd been lads together.

Walter finished his basket and got up to go. He was to take the donkey carts over the cliffs to fetch the bait that was gathered. He said he must round up some of the lads to help him. I wished I could have gone too, but I was needed at home, so I sat tight.

Miriam came out onto her front to get a bit of sun while she did her knitting. Miriam had no husband and no son, but every spare moment she was knitting away at a gansey. It was never for a particular person, just a medium-sized gansey for whoever needed it most. Miriam did all the things that any mother did, though she'd no children of her own. It was as though the whole village were her children. Old or young, she mothered us all; I can't think how we'd have managed without her.

She did well enough living by herself and though she wasn't rich, she didn't lack for anything either. Sometimes we paid her for her simples and her nursing care, but if folk were short they'd pay her with fish or by helping with repairs to her neat cottage on the front. However poor they were, none got turned away from her door.

I watched her knitting in the sun and wondered if I dare ask her about William and the dreadful thing that had happened. There was nobody else around and I could see that she wasn't busy for once. Still I was reluctant; you didn't call on Miriam unless something was really up – sickness or childbirth or death. You didn't call to pass the time of day, but the strange thing was that Miriam looked up and beckoned me.

I went over to her gate.

"Well, Liza Welford, so you're left to mind your Billy."

She continued with her knitting while she spoke, bony fingers working fast, not needing to look at what she did … like all the women in our bay.

"Aye," I answered. "We've set them on their way."

I couldn't think when I'd looked close at Miriam before, she never stopped still long enough as a rule. Fine wrinkles creased her forehead and cheeks. Her hair worn thin and silver was tucked neatly beneath her blue cotton Sandwick

bonnet. Light grey eyes peered sharp at me through small gold-rimmed spectacles.

"You'll be missing your Esther, I dare say?"

"Aye," I repeated it with a sigh.

"She were right fond of you," said Miriam, "and you'll miss her sore, but you must treasure what you remember and that way you'll still have her."

I nodded. She was right, but there was something more I needed to ask.

"That night," I said. "That night when Grandma Esther died, she tried to tell me something. It was about my mam. She tried to tell how Mam's young brother William Archer was drowned."

Miriam's head jerked up and the wrinkles in her forehead gathered tighter still, but she nodded me to have my say.

"Well … she never got it said, but I've asked Aunt Hannah and she's told me what a terrible thing it was and how it'd upset my mam, but she didn't know what happened when they went off looking. She said it was you who brought Mam back."

"So I did and there's no mystery as to where she was. She was here in my cottage till late that night, though as for what went on … that's between her and me."

Miriam folded her knitting and got up from her chair. I thought she was sending me off. I thought I'd pried where I shouldn't and was ready to go, but Miriam pointed to Billy, who'd been slinging pebbles against her wall.

"Fetch your Billy through to my garden, then you may take a drink of tea with me."

CHAPTER SEVEN

It was a special treat to go into Miriam's garden and Billy came willingly enough. It spread a long way up onto the hillside from the back of her cottage; the biggest garden in the village, packed with herbs and flowers. There was lavender to crush and sniff, and liquorice root to clean and chew. I led Billy through Miriam's kitchen that was hung with bunches of herbs drying for the winter use. I would have liked to go out with him into the garden, but there were more important things to worry about.

Miriam put on her kettle and made me sit. A proper visitor I was and I wasn't used to it. She brought our tea and sat beside her fire, thoughtful for a moment, then she spoke.

"I'll tell what I think I should, though I'll not tell all. No one will ever know it all but your mam and me."

I nodded, feeling the importance of what she said.

"It's a long way back now, but it's one of those days that stick in your memory. You'd like to forget it, but you can't. I was here, busy with something – I can't think what. I knew there'd been a commotion on the beach. I didn't go out, I knew they'd call me soon enough if I was needed. I looked out once, I recall, and saw Martha down there by herself, but I thought nowt of that. Then I glanced out a while later and there she was in exactly the same spot. She'd never moved and the tide was coming in. The second time I looked something bothered me, something about the stillness of her, and I decided to go down.

"I passed someone on the way and I heard that William was lost and that they were all searching for him. When I got closer to Martha, I really took fright. I could see that she'd not moved, not one speck, and the sea was up to her knees … her face blank, like a person dead. I ran and took hold of her, but she was stiff and cold, staring out to sea, and her just a young girl like you."

When Miriam told me that I bit my lips hard to keep back the tears. I knew I was being told something very secret. I must treat it with respect.

"I could tell what had happened," said Miriam. "I knew when I saw her face that William had drowned and that what she wanted was to rush into the sea and follow him, but fear stopped her. So there she stood, letting the sea come up to her. She couldn't go to meet it, but she couldn't resign herself to living either. Aye," said Miriam, tapping me on the arm, "you let the tears fall, for it was a thing no young girl should have to face."

I did as she said; I let the tears fall and wept for my mam and her brother. When I'd dried my eyes and calmed myself, Miriam finished her telling.

"I got her to move, though it was difficult, but somehow I got her back up here and she stayed with me for the rest of the day. Outside they were searching for William still, but I knew it was in vain. William was beyond any help, it was Martha who needed me. We talked and talked and I'll not say all, but a struggle took place and by the time night came, Martha had somehow found the strength to go on with her life. It was with grim determination though and she was never a child again, not after that.

"Now Liza," she said, putting her hands on my shoulders to make me really take notice, "I've said what I thought right and what Esther in her wisdom wanted you to know, but the time will come when you must speak to your mam. That would be for the best."

It left me quiet and sad, almost wishing I'd never asked. I thanked her and called our Billy in from the garden.

I thought about my talk with Miriam all night and couldn't sleep. I didn't think I'd ever be able to speak to Mam about what happened, for her hard shell was as strong as the flithers' shell. You could never break through that.

I got up early next morning and by the time Mam and Irene arrived back from spending the night with cousin Rachel in Whitby, I'd polished the fireplace and side oven and covered the table with oilskins, for it was too cold to get the baiting done outside that day. We disliked that, for it meant our only living room cluttered and mucky with it all, but we'd no choice. I'd filled the buckets ready to soak the shelled limpets and mussels and got the skeps out, with two lines all cleaned and a kettle boiling ready to make their tea.

Mam and Irene were tired, but they smiled real surprised when they saw the work I'd done.

"I do believe our Liza's growing up," said Mam. That was compliment enough from her.

I made tea and we all gathered round the table to start shelling. I was needed to help as they'd such a load to do and the next day's supply was to be kept fresh by changing the water and fetching seaweed to cover the bucket tops.

There came a knock at the door and I went to open it. A young postboy held out a parcel addressed to me. He touched his cap and pushed the parcel into my arms.

"Special delivery, miss. I'm to wait on a reply – a message for the picture man in Whitby."

Mam and Irene came to see what was up.

"Well fancy," said Irene. "Fancy our Liza getting a parcel. Get it opened, lass."

My hands shook as I fiddled with the string. It was tightly knotted, but we couldn't cut it, for it was a good useful bit of string. At last Mam wiped her hands down her apron and took it from me. Her strong fingers quickly teased the knot apart and a beautiful new book was discovered, bound with green linen and stamped with gold lettering. A real treasure, this. I picked it up and read out loud: "*In Exchange For A Soul* by Mary Linskill."

Mam looked at me, pleased and wondering. "He's sent you a book, Liza. He must have thought you a clever lass."

"Nay," I said. "It's that gossiping Mary Jane. She told him how Miss Hindmarch wished me back in school."

Irene stroked the clean new cover. "Oh Liza … it's beautiful. There's nobody in the bay has a book like it."

Mam held up a handwritten sheet for me to read.

"See what it says here, Liza, for this lad's waiting to take a reply."

I read it carefully to myself.

"Come on, Liza," said Irene. "Tell us what it says."

"You'll never believe," I said. "He invites Miss Liza Welford and Miss Mary Jane Ruswarp, along with any members of their families, to visit his photographic studio in Whitby. We're to view our picture, which is enlarged and on display as it has won a prize in a national photographic competition."

"Never," said Mam.

"What," said Irene. "A picture of them two cheeky things! I cannot think that's right."

"Well, it's true enough," I said, though I could hardly think it myself, that scared and excited I felt. "He says we may go next Saturday if that's to our convenience and he'll provide a pony and trap for our transportation. Well Mam, what do you say to that?"

Mam was speechless, but she eventually believed it and we sent the postboy back with the message that we'd be pleased to go.

I couldn't really settle down to the caving after that. Dad came to help, as he'd not been out during the night and we needed all the help we could get. When he heard the news, he was that tickled he kept looking at me and saying, "Well, our Liza, a prize-winning picture? Well, our Liza, who's a fine lady now?" He laughed and smiled as he hadn't done since Grandma Esther died.

No matter how I tried I couldn't concentrate on the shelling and Mam let me off. I ran down to the Ruswarps' with the news, for I was bursting to tell Mary Jane and Mam said she'd get on better without me.

Mary Jane threw herself on the floor, laughing and laughing, till Mrs Ruswarp got worried. It was only when I showed the letter that she calmed down and they both believed me.

We talked of nothing else that week and made such preparations for our outing. Mam with her canny ways insisted that we should make it our shopping day for the wedding and save ourselves the expense of another trip. As the transport was to be provided we could all go – Mam, Dad, Irene, Mrs Ruswarp, Mary Jane and me. We'd been worried about Grandpa, but as usual Miriam came to our rescue. She said she'd look after Billy and take Grandpa his meals. We were excited and it was only the thought of Grandpa's unhappiness that marred our pleasure.

We'd tried so hard to cheer him and get him to take interest again, but nothing roused him. Not Irene's wedding, not our prize picture, not the coming bairn.

I kept my book in our loft in a fine woven basket that Grandma Esther had made for me one Eastertide. I'd never had a book. There were books at school, but they were worn and had to be shared and only for use in school time. Then we had our family bible, our family record of births and deaths, which Dad kept in a special chest. This beautiful bound book was quite different, a special book of my own. No one in the bay had such a thing. I don't think I'd ever have tried to read it if it wasn't that the picture man had written a special message inside it.

The first night that I had it, I carried my candle up to bed and looked again at my new treasure. I opened the cover and saw the picture man's writing. I thought, fancy doing that. Fancy writing in a brand-new book, on such a fresh white page. It said: For Liza, hoping that within these pages she will discover that learning can be for her. I was puzzled, I didn't know what it meant. I remembered how I'd told him 'learning had nowt to do with me', then worried that I'd been rude. Still, rudeness or not, it had brought me this book. He means me to read it, I thought. I'd have to be very careful if I were to read it. I wouldn't have to dirty these crisp pages or mark the cover. I'd have to scrub my hands real well if I were to read it.

I turned the pages delicately, past the Contents and on to the story. I glanced at each page as I passed, then stopped. I stared at the title of Chapter Two: *A North Yorkshire Fisher Maiden*. Fisher maidens, I thought. Why, who'd put them in a book? I looked down the page and began to read.

A group of tall, handsome fisher-girls who were down by the edge of the tide – such girls as you would hardly see anywhere else in England for strength and straightness, for roundness of form and bright, fresh healthfulness of countenance.

Why, I thought, it's about girls like us … like me or Irene or Mary Jane.

I read on and found more to interest me. It was about a fisher-girl called Barbara Burdas, who'd two young men both loving her, one of them a fisherman named David Andoe and the other was Hartas Theyn, a rather shabby squire's son.

I turned back to the beginning and started to read it properly. I'd never read anything like it before. It was a love story but very sad, with things going wrong. Dreadful things happened to Barbara Burdas, but then such things happened in our own bay, I knew that well enough. I read and read until my candle guttered and Irene came grumbling up to bed, fishing around in the dark.

CHAPTER EIGHT

We'd all dressed smart on the Saturday morning, scrubbed clean and wearing our Sunday best. Mam and Irene in their silk bonnets and me and Mary Jane laced tight in our best boots. The pony and trap arrived on time and we climbed in chatting and smiling at the treat of it all.

John Ruswarp came to set us off on our way. He'd have liked to be coming but wasn't allowed, for he mustn't see the stuffs for our wedding clothes – bad luck that would be. John ran beside us as the trap set off. He ran till he could keep up no more, with Irene waving and blushing till he was out of sight.

We enjoyed the drive into Whitby, passing through villages we knew well, holding our heads high, giggling as folk turned to watch, wondering what was up.

Whitby was always busy on a Saturday, what with the street traders and the market and the ladies and gentlemen buying their goods. We went straight to the photographic studios, for we couldn't wait to see our picture. The studio had a double shop front, new and grand, with flowers and plants arranged in the windows and flower designs on the glass, with dark velvet curtains behind.

We went in and stood shy and uncomfortable in the waiting room, staring at the leather upholstery and rich drapes. A lady sat there with her child and its nurse, all dressed very fine. The lady wore a cream dress with lace and tucks and a row of bows to show off her tiny waist. The nurse was dressed in black and white, but the best silk. I felt sorry for the baby; its fat cheeks bulged and it fretted and peered from beneath a bonnet that was so bedecked with lace and frills that the poor bairn could hardly see.

I tried not to stare, but that was hard for I wanted to remember it all. The lady fetched out a tiny lace handkerchief when we came in. She held it to her nose, turning her head to whisper to the nurse as if she thought us most inferior – and us all scrubbed and in our finery.

I was glad when the picture man came through to us and greeted us real pleased and polite, ignoring the lady with her miserable child. He invited us upstairs to another room and there on the wall in a carved wooden frame hung the picture of me and Mary Jane. At the sight of it we lost all shyness and talked and laughed. The picture was so full of life, you'd think we could've jumped up at any moment and splashed away into the sea.

The picture man said that he was very proud that we'd won him a prize in such an important competition. He brought out two smaller prints of our picture that he'd set in neat frames and he gave them to us to hang on the wall at home.

Mam said as how it was so kind of the picture man to have sent me such a lovely book.

"But did you read it, young lady?" he asked.

Well, once he'd got me going on that, I talked on and on, telling how I'd read it once and then read it again. How I'd told the story to Mary Jane and then how Mam and Irene had let me sit up late each night, reading the story out loud to them and how we'd all thought the story wonderful and sad and how we felt flat now that we were getting near to the end, and thinking we'd have to start at the beginning again.

"I thought it might be just the thing," he said. "Do you know of Mary Linskill, the lady who wrote the story? A Whitby lady she was, though sadly she died a few years back."

"Whitby?" I said. "Did she really live in Whitby? Did you know her?" The picture man smiled at my surprise. "I did indeed," he said.

Mam and Dad and the others stood quiet and smiling, letting me chatter on and on about my wonderful book. The picture man was pleased, I could tell, pleased that he'd found something that had given such pleasure and interest.

"I have to make a photograph of a baby now," he said, "but when I've done, I could show you where Mary lived and tell you more about her."

I was delighted at that, but Mam said though it was most kind, he shouldn't waste his valuable time.

No, he insisted, he'd enjoy doing that, so we arranged to meet him in the market place at noon.

Mam explained that we'd shopping to do for Irene's wedding. The picture man congratulated Irene, making her blush, then he said he'd like to make a studio portrait of her, for she'd a striking face. That made her blush even more.

We swept through the waiting room, our noses in the air.

"They'll see our picture when they go through," Mary Jane whispered.

Our bridesmaids' shopping was soon done. We'd got a smooth white silk for our dresses, with lace to stitch at the necks; a yard of blue velvet ribbon each for our sashes and new white stockings to go with our white boots.

"We'll be fine as any lady," said Mary Jane.

Irene couldn't make up her mind about the stuff for her dress, so we left her with Mam and Mrs Ruswarp and went with Dad to the market place. We loved going to look at the stalls and Dad let us sit up at the counter of Jacksons, beneath the cheerful striped awnings. We both had a penny lick piled high with hokey-pokey ice cream, a rare treat that froze our tongues and made our teeth ache as we crunched the tiny slivers of ice. It was finished all too soon and we handed the little glass holders back to Mr Jackson, to be dipped into a bucket of hot water for cleaning and then set up on the stall again.

Dad was in a grand mood, calling out to his Whitby friends that he hadn't seen for a time, passing on the latest gossip, telling everyone about our prize-winning photograph and worrying over the news from South Africa. There were rumours of sickness and fever there, and our lads suffering from poor rations. Many folk were saying that they ought to be brought back home.

When we all met up again, Irene had found the material she liked, and ribbons and lace to make it bonny. The picture man found us by the fish stall that belonged to Hannah Smith, who we all called Trickey. Mrs Smith had a reputation for being able to sell fish to anyone, so crafty and clever she was.

"You shouldn't stand talking too long to Mrs Smith," said the picture man, "she'll talk you into buying a haddock to take back to Sandwick Bay."

We followed the picture man up Church Street, then off to the right through one of the narrow dark alleys that open into a yard, Blackburn's Yard, just like ours, built into the hillside, but a little longer than our own.

"She never lived here?" I said. "Not that lady who wrote the story?"

"Yes," said the picture man. He pointed out a small cottage. "This is where she was born and this," he said, pointing to a rather newer cottage, "this is where the family moved to later."

"But was she not rich and clever?" I asked.

"She was clever enough, but she was never rich."

"Is that so?" said Mam. "She wrote that lovely book, but never had money?"

"Her father was one of the constables," said the picture man. "A respectable working man. Sometimes, when he

53

took female prisoners, he would keep them in the cottage with his family. Mary had the job of carrying the food to them. I think she often heard their sad stories. A strange start in life, I should think."

Mam nodded her head. "Strange indeed."

"But how did she get to write her stories?" I asked.

"Ah well, young lady, she went to school. Her mam was keen for her to do that, so she went to school and she worked really hard."

"Where did she go to school?" I asked.

"Here, in Whitby, a school like yours no doubt, though I don't believe she had anyone as kind as Miss Hindmarch for her teacher."

"But when did she write her stories?"

"Ah, that was later. She worked as a milliner at first … then she became a governess and spent many years away from Whitby. It was in her middle years that she returned to Whitby and set about earning her living from writing her stories. After her father died she tried to keep her mother and sister with what she earned. Those were very hard times for Mary."

"Did she not earn money from her books?"

"Not at first. Often she became so short of money that there was little food in the house. Mary would dread her friends visiting, for she had nothing to offer them. Sometimes she could not walk out for she'd no boots to wear."

That shocked me, for no visitor at our cottage would ever go short of food and though a fisher-girl like me might go barefoot on the sand, no decent person could walk through town without boots.

"Her friends lost patience with her at times," he said, though he smiled as he remembered it. "They thought she was mad to be trying to write, when she could have earned a respectable living as a governess. That would have been more seemly, more ladylike."

The picture man laughed, but I could tell that he admired Mary's stubbornness. "Mary was determined," he said, "and she succeeded in the end."

"So she did get to be rich?" said Mam.

"No, but she managed to buy a house up in Springvale, on the smarter side of town, and she lived there with her mother, but sadly it was not long before she died. It is only now that her books are selling well. I'm sorry that Mary never lived to enjoy it."

We all stood quiet, struck by the shame of it all.

"But now, young lady," said the picture man, "I have another gift that I hope you will all enjoy."

From his pocket he took another book, just as beautifully bound as the first. My mouth dropped open and my hands went out.

"Well," said Irene. "Two books, two books. I've never heard the like."

"*The Haven Under the Hill*" I read from the stamped gold title letters. "It's by Mary, too. Oh I can't wait to start to read it."

Mam and Dad were overwhelmed and they couldn't thank him enough. I forgot my manners and opened the book, pointing out words to Mary Jane. "Why, it's about Whitby, this is. It tells about Hild and Caedmon and the Abbey and the old street round the corner that we still call Haggerlythe."

I'd been so excited, that the time had flown by. We realized that we needed to find the pony and trap again and set off back to Sandwick Bay.

We were tired after our busy day, though we were laughing and chattering all the way and I clutched tight to my precious book. A chill wind came off the sea and the sinking sun painted patterns over the hills and valleys. When we reached the top of our steep bank, we fell silent. There was John Ruswarp waiting for us by the stile, where the heather begins. There was another young man with him, a man I didn't recognise, tall and thin and sunburnt, dressed in Army clothes.

We stared, but Mam climbed down from the trap. She stretched up her hands to the strange young man, touching his cheek.

"Our Frank," she said.

I couldn't believe it was our Frank. I don't know how Mam managed to recognise him straight off like that. It was more than eighteen months since he'd gone off to the fighting, but I would never have thought a lad could change so much in that time.

He'd always been strong and healthy, had our Frank, with his blue eyes and ruddy cheeks. Well built he'd been, with good muscles. It had been no effort to him to heave a coble up onto the sands, or swing a little lass up into the air. This man was pitifully thin, his cheeks sallow beneath the sunburn and his thick golden hair bleached white and sparse.

John came to help Irene down from the trap. I think he'd been shocked too when Frank turned up knocking at the Ruswarps' door, after he'd got no reply from our cottage. Irene went up to Frank and hugged him, the tears pouring down her face.

"Our Frank ... our Frank," she said.

It was Dad who voiced what was on all our minds. He followed Irene down and took Frank by the hand when Mam moved back, then he clapped his arm round Frank's shoulder, hugging the thin trembling body to his chest.

"Eeeh lad ... what ails? Are you hurt?"

Frank clung to my dad for a moment as though he were a bairn, but then he pulled back, showing us he'd still got some pride.

"I've been sick, that's all. I've had the fever like a lot of them, but I'm better now. Nay," he said, coming over to me, "this grand lady is never our Liza? Have you not a kiss for your brother?"

I had felt shy, him looking so different and all, but it was his own cheeky way of talking and I threw my arms around him, though I didn't like the bony feel of his shoulders beneath the army jacket.

"I cannot swing you up onto my shoulder, such a fine grown lady you are," he said, and though they laughed, Mam's lips tightened and I knew she thought that he'd not have the strength to do it either.

We let the pony and trap go back to Whitby and we all walked down the steep hill to Sandwick, carrying our parcels. We'd much to tell Frank, both happy and sad, and we talked till late at night.

Frank only had a few days' leave, then he had to get back to Scarborough where he was billeted. He'd not been able to come back in August with the others as he'd been so ill. He made light of his sickness but the weakness and fits of trembling that came over him told us that he'd been very ill indeed. There was a great deal of talking done, but most of it was on our side. Try as he might, Dad could not get Frank to tell what he'd been doing, away at the war. Once Mam tried to get him to say, but all he'd answer was that he was shamed to speak of it, and begged her not to ask.

Frank spent much of his time sitting beside Grandpa's bed. I don't think they did much talking, but they seemed to have a quiet understanding. Billy ran to hide whenever Frank looked his way.

The night before Frank was due to return, Irene came up late to bed. She'd been sitting out on the top staithe with Frank and John, all talking softly together, though Mam kept saying that they'd all be getting chilled. Irene lay beside me quietly sobbing; I could feel the heaving of her shoulders and hear the catch of her breath.

"What is it?" I asked.

"'Tis nowt," she said. "Nowt, but Frank has talked John into giving up his plans for the Army."

"What? Are you not glad of that? You didn't want him going off?"

"Oh I'm glad all right. I'm that relieved I can't say how much, but it's what Frank said that's shaken me. It's bad out there, where the fighting is, much worse than we thought. Frank says he's shamed to speak of it to Mam and Dad, but he managed to tell John, for he couldn't bear to let John follow him."

"Well," I said. "All that fighting and killing must be dreadful, but why is he so shamed? Soldiers are supposed to fight, aren't they?"

"Aye, but Frank says it's the women and children involved in it all that he cannot feel right about. He says they've found many a farmhouse with the men away fighting and they've turned out the mother and her bairns and they've had orders to burn the place to the ground. They've burnt everything – their food, their clothes – and left them with nowt but what they stand in."

"Nay," I said, "but what happens to them?"

"He says they're herded away into camps, where they live in tents, cramped together, sleeping on the ground. They've nowt to drink but fever-ridden water. They cannot keep themselves clean and they've very little food. They're dying in those camps, he says, mothers and bairns, dying like flies."

I was silent then. I couldn't see how a decent lad like our Frank could be part of all that, then I realised that since he'd volunteered himself he'd no choice but to do it or be killed.

We all went up to the top of the bank to set Frank on his way, but we were quiet. His homecoming hadn't been the happy one we'd wanted. Mam clung to him when it was time to go and Dad told him that his lines would still be waiting, and then we had to let him go on his way.

I sat on Plosher Rock, staring out to sea, watching the wake of the boats till they vanished. Nearby, the waves burst white and fizzing, lapping at the driftwood beyond my feet. Far out, the swell was dark blue, patterned like mackerel skin with the lighter blue of the sky. All heaving gently in a quiet breathing rhythm … just a light stirring here and there, a hint of the power beneath.

The low sun warmed my back and apart from the guilt of knowing there was work to be done and the unspoken chiding that'd come from Mam, I was happy. Content to sit for the moment.

The weeks had passed and we were well into November, though the weather had stayed fine for that time of year. Irene's dress was ready and beautiful, hanging from the beam in our loft. My dress just needed the lace and frill, and we'd been to chapel to hear the banns being read. Mam and Mrs Ruswarp had been sitting up late into the night, getting all the stitching done, while I read to them from *The Haven Under the Hill*. We all enjoyed the story just as much as the first one and I often thought about the Whitby woman who'd written it. Irene was happy and looking forward; she was even looking forward to her baby being born, though I couldn't understand that. Still, I loved the thought of being an auntie … I had such plans: I'd make little presents, I'd carve a boat out of wood, the way I'd seen Grandpa do it.

I sat there thinking about it all, but then noticed the sky changing. Grey clouds heavy with rain came over from the horizon, heading inland, though the sun still shone through, sharp and red, in spiky rays. The clouds came over very sudden and it went dark and cold. I saw red flecks of the sun's reflection in the nearest waves. I shuddered. Flecked with blood, I thought. Great spots of rain began to fall as I ran home thinking of my dad out there on the sea.

It was late that night that the storm really broke. I couldn't remember another storm like it. Mam had sent me and Irene up to bed but we couldn't sleep, what with worrying about Dad and John who were both out in it all. We heard footsteps passing to and fro beneath our window and a lot of shouting going on. At last we heard our own door slam hard, caught in the wind ... we knew Mam had gone out.

"I'll not lie abed in this," said Irene and she was up and pulling on her frock that was so tight now and wrapping her shawl criss-cross, to fasten at the back. I couldn't stop her so I helped her, then dressed myself as well. I followed her down the ladder, past Billy rolling around in Mam's bed. He jumped out when he saw us and pattered downstairs behind us, his thin legs bare beneath his white shirt.

"Get back, get back," we told him, but he followed and we couldn't make him stay.

The blast was so strong, we couldn't get the door open at first, then when we did, it slammed back so sharp our Billy screamed. He wasn't caught by it, just scared, and I got hold of him, suddenly scared myself. Mam came running up and pushed us back inside. She was soaked and her hair all snarzly. I thought she'd shout at us for coming out, but the tense, low voice she spoke with frightened me more.

"We'll have to get the boat out," she said. "We must help fetch the men. Irene, you run to the Pickerings'. Liza, keep Billy here ... keep him safe for me."

Then she was gone and Irene after her with the door banging and banging till I caught it on the sneck. Billy was white and shivering so I took him back upstairs and crept into Mam's bed beside him. I cuddled up and he fell asleep.

I couldn't sleep though and I wondered about Grandpa – surely he couldn't be sleeping through all this commotion. I got up and made some tea and carried a cup into him. He lay on his back, staring wide-eyed at the ceiling. I put the cup beside him.

"There's a terrible storm, Grandpa. They're wanting to get the boat out."

He never moved or spoke and I went back to Billy. I sat full-dressed on the edge of Mam's bed. I hated sitting there, I wanted to be out and seeing what was going on. Then Irene came back, puffing and blowing, stamping frantic up our stairs, straight into Grandpa's room.

"You must come," she cried. "You must come. We've no men, they're all out there, beyond the bay, and they cannot bring the boats in."

I followed her into his room. She ran round his bed, pulling at the blankets, her hair streaming water, sprinkling wet over the sheets.

"They'll be lost if you don't come," but Grandpa stared blank at her.

Then Mam came flying up the stairs as drenched as Irene.

"I cannot move him," Irene's voice rose. "I cannot make him come."

Mam stood at the foot of his bed and spoke again in that strained, quiet voice.

"We cannot launch the boat without you be coxswain. Get out of your bed, Isaac Welford, and think what your Esther would have said."

I'd never heard Mam speak so sharp to him before and I caught my breath at it, but Grandpa looked at Mam and I could tell he'd understood and listened to what she'd said.

Then he spoke at last. "Who is there to crew?"

"There's Walter Snaith and his grandson, there's John Pickering and old Tom Danby and a gang of lads all willing to row, but there's none as knows the sandbanks and the rocks, there's none as can guide her out but you."

Still Grandpa shook his head. "Nay. They're only old fellas and young lads and it'll take every one of them. There's none left to launch her."

"We can launch her," said Irene. "Us women can do the launching."

Grandpa shook his head again. "Women? It takes strong men to launch that boat. Aye, and plenty of 'em."

"Hannah knows what to do. She's helped before," Irene insisted.

"Nay, we've never had women in those racks. Ye'd not stand a chance."

Irene covered her face with her hands, near despairing.

Mam spoke firm again. "Now listen you here, Isaac Welford. If you can be coxswain and those lads can man her, then we women can launch her."

At last Grandpa seemed to gather himself together. A spark of his old self gleamed in his face and he laughed out loud.

"All right, my lass, all right. If you lot can launch her, then we will man her. Now get me out of this bed."

He held up his arms and Mam and Irene grabbed hold and pulled him out. Mam picked up his gansey from the dresser and eased it over his nightshirt.

"Fetch Dan's spare, Liza, and his oilskins, too."

I ran back to Mam's room and fetched my dad's gear and watched as they got Grandpa dressed. He was shaky and stiff-legged – he'd not been out of his bed for weeks – but he bellowed questions at Mam and she answered fast and clear. Then off they went, Grandpa stumping down our stairs, and I turned back to Billy.

He was awake and out of bed and I wasn't going to stay at home, not now. I got Billy's coat and wrapped him up good and warm, pushing on his boots. "You stay by me," I said. "You stay by me whatever happens."

Billy nodded, his eyes wide and round.

CHAPTER TEN

The wind was so strong that it was hard to breathe at first and I nearly turned round and went back inside. Such a rush there was, folk shouting and surging like a great wave down to the boathouse. I grabbed our Billy tight and we became part of the wave, down the staithe and onto the beach we went.

They'd already got the lights out, big cans with a paraffin light that we call ducks. They'd carried them down the lifeboat ramp where they lit up the beach.

The sun was just beginning to show and a dim grey light lit the sea. The sea as I'd never seen it before. Our bay was filled with white foam, seething like a boiling cauldron, the white only broken by grey breakers that turned black as they burst, sending creamy spray flying high into the sky. I turned my head sharp, catching rainbow flashes from the corners of my eyes, and far out were glimpses of dark shapes that vanished, then reappeared: our small fishing fleet, so tossed that you couldn't see them clear.

Billy snatched at my hand, pointing and shouting with delight. I turned to see them pulling open the doors of the lifeboat house and the great shining prow of our lifeboat gleaming in the light of the ducks. Our lifeboat that we loved, even worshipped – the spirit of our village, as near a holy thing as we could have.

The boat was full of young lads and the boathouse full of women. Mam helped Grandpa up the ladder and she and Hannah half-lifted, half-threw him into the stern. Some of the lads who'd come to row were swamped in their dads' oilskins, but the scratch crew were all in place. Grandpa gave the signal to Walter Snaith who fired the warning pistol. Mam and Hannah and the other women gathered round the winch, as many as could find a place to hold, and Irene let loose the safety chain. Slowly, bit by bit and jerking to the side, the boat was lowered onto its carriage, then steered out onto the ramp.

"Away … let her away," shouted Grandpa and our great boat rumbled down the slipway, coming to rest steady on its carriage on the sand.

Then came the launchers' hardest part. The women formed up in the launching racks, two by two, ready to push her out to the sea. Hannah stood at the front shouting instructions and I saw that Mary Jane had gone to pull on the ropes with other girls and lads.

"Right," I said to Billy. "We're needed."

I ran, pulling Billy with me, and grabbed the rope beside Mary Jane.

"You get that rope and you pull hard," I yelled at him.

I saw Mam in one of the racks, straining with the weight, then Irene slotted herself in behind. I could see that bothered Mam, she was worrying about Irene and her bairn, but strong arms pulled Irene from the rack and a great powerful body took her place. It was Nelly Wright and I could have hugged her. Irene didn't stay to argue, but went to push at the back.

The women strained, but the boat didn't move.

"I'll call," shouted Hannah. "One, two and away. One, two and away."

I think every person in our bay was there, everyone who could stand. I saw Mary Jane's granny and Old Miriam hauling on the ropes, and Annie Lythe, who'd no family to save, was there with her oldest lad Robbie and lanky Dory too, pulling and heaving with the rest. At last the carriage shifted a bit and a cheer went up from the lads above. Once it started it moved slow but steady across the sand till we neared the water's edge.

We dropped our ropes then and ran to push at the back. I lost Billy at that moment, but I didn't stop to think, just ran and pushed with the others, pushed for all I was worth. The women in the racks trudged out into the waves.

I hardly noticed when we first reached the sea. My skirts were so drenched and cold that the water made no difference, but when we got further out I knew all right, for a wicked underswell pulled at me, trying to pluck my feet from under my legs. It caught me and I fell; the freezing salt waves punched me in the face. I was left wallowing as the others went on. Such a rage of anger rose in me that I dragged myself upright, shouting and screaming abuse – abuse at the sea, shaking my fists, tears bursting from my eyes.

Then I stopped. Pushing ahead was Mam, past her waist in the swirling mass. My mam, who was so feared of the sea that she couldn't cross a causeway, couldn't bear to wet her toes. I didn't know how she was doing it, wading out like that. And what of Irene, following on behind, with that little baby growing inside her, the one I'd be an auntie for. I remembered Billy; that was my job. If Billy got lost or hurt it'd be my fault. I turned back to look for him.

Billy was hiding beside the lifeboat ramp and he'd found his friend Jackie Lythe. I suppose they thought they'd got a bit of shelter from the wind, but they were both shivering down there.

"Get 'em up and make 'em run." It was Miriam, who stood beside me pointing her bony finger at the two lads. "Get 'em out. They can run with the ropes now. They're coming away from the racks and we'll all be needed again."

So I made Billy and Jackie go back down the beach. Mam and Irene and the others were coming towards us through the waves. Two of the lads climbed over the sides of the boat and untied the launching ropes, flinging them down to Hannah below.

We all had to get ready now for the last big haul. The ropes had to be dragged along the beach either way and tugged real sharp, to catapult the lifeboat from its carriage, forward into the sea. We all waited on Grandpa's signal, for he had to choose just the right moment – when a wave had gone, but before the next one came.

"Away now … away," came the cry. We took hold and pulled and shouted, till we were running fast.

"Away now. Away!" we yelled, as though the strength of our voices would add to the weight on the ropes. Billy hauled in front of me. He was running so fast I swear his feet never touched the ground, but swung to and fro. I didn't see that I was running into a rock and I fell hard, rolling quick to the side, for I knew I'd be trampled if I didn't shift.

I rolled on the sand as the cry changed.

"She's off." The rope fell slack as the boat plunged forward into the waves, the oars pulling back, not quite together but strong enough to move her, dipping sharp, up and down.

It was Billy who found me then. I heard his voice. "Liza, Liza," and I shouted back to him.

"I thought you'd got squashed," he said.

"I'm worse than squashed," I said. "Pull me up. We must find our mam."

I wasn't the only one who'd fallen; there were women helping each other up and rubbing knees and shins, all along the beach. We gathered together by the ducks. They gave little heat, but they seemed to give a bit of comfort. Hannah said that the bairns and the old ones should all go home, as there was no more we could do, but none would go. We huddled together, watching the heavy boat that looked so fragile now, swinging up and down and out of sight. Giving us a glimpse, then nowt.

Mam rubbed Irene's hands. "Get yourself back," she said. "Get yourself back and into your bed."

"I'll not … not till they're fetched."

"They're doing grand," said Mam. "Who'd have thought those lads could row like that? They look to have reached the bank and be getting through."

We all looked, narrowing our eyes. The bank was the dangerous shallows at the mouth of our bay.

"There's none but Isaac Welford could have taken them through," said Hannah.

We waited helpless and dreary, but still no one would go home. Now we'd done our work and the effort was over, the freezing cold and wet made itself felt. The children began their shivering.

"Jump up and down," said Miriam. "Ye'll catch your deaths if ye stand there gawping. You show them, Liza, and you, Mary Jane. Jump about and clap your hands."

We tried, but we were too cold to get going properly.

"Ye must," said Miriam. "Ye'll freeze solid else. Ye'll turn into breakwaters, everyone of you, stuck for ever ont' beach."

So we laughed and tried again. Mary Jane started chanting a skipping rhyme:

"Souther wind souther,
Bring father home to mother."

"That's it, lass," Miriam said. "They all know that," and she joined in, jumping up and down, her sodden skirts flapping round her skinny legs:

"Souther wind souther,
Bring father home to mother."

Soon we were all at it, jumping to the rhythm, clapping hands, shouting as loud as we could. We went on to another rhyme:

"Northern sea, silver sea,
Bring my daddy back to me,
Hush the waves and still the sea,
And bring my daddy back to me."

All the mams joined in, bellowing it out faster and faster, and it warmed us and cheered us, till the cry went up.

"They're coming back!"

We stopped our jumping and ran to the water's edge, but we could see nothing clear. We waited in silence then, watching and screwing up our eyes. I thought I saw a moving shape, then it vanished, then I saw it again.

At last we could see that a small boat, tossing fiercely, was heading steadily for the shore. Then we saw another behind it.

"The cobles!" shouted Hannah, and a great cheer went up.

We couldn't see the lifeboat, but the small boats, taking courage from the lifeboat standing by, were coming in one by one. When the lifeboat did at last come into view there was more cheering and clapping of hands, but Mam and me stood next to Hannah.

"What is it?" said Mam. She knew Hannah of old.

Hannah shook her head. "There's not all there should be."

As the cobles came in we spread out along the beach to help drag them up. I kept looking for Dad, but I couldn't see him.

When the lifeboat neared the shore we saw that it pulled a coble fastened by a line, and another upturned hull dragged behind that. I pulled at Mam's arm.

"Look," I said. "It's Dad's boat tied up behind. It's the *Sneaton Lass*."

Mam didn't move. The women gathered together to help get the boat out of the water. Irene came with Mrs Ruswarp and Mary Jane following.

"We cannot see the *Lily Belle*," Irene said. Then she followed Mam's gaze to the upturned hull dragged behind our *Sneaton Lass*.

"No," she whispered. "No."

Mam seemed to shake herself and put her arms round Irene. "You'll see. He'll be in the lifeboat, him and your dad. There's a line fastened. We'll find them in the boat."

We went down to help carry the ropes up to the winch. The men and lads were jumping over the sides into the shallows and the ones who'd fetched their cobles in came to help. The lifeboat was hauled back out of the water a deal more easily than she'd gone in.

We saw Dad inside the boat, but we couldn't see John. Uncle Jack was there and Sam Ruswarp; that made me think that John must be there too. Dad jumped over the edge and splashed towards us, but as he came near we saw that his face was grim and he slowed as though he didn't wish to reach us. He looked at Irene and Mrs Ruswarp, shaking his head.

"I'm sorry, lass," he said.

Sam Ruswarp came up behind them, hanging back from his mam as though shamed. But Mrs Ruswarp threw her arms round him and Mary Jane clung to them both.

Irene stared at Dad.

"Nay, nay … I've seen him. Look, he's there," she said, pointing to the lifeboat. "He's there in the boat. I saw his gansey. I know it well. I knitted it myself, the waves and herring-bone … I'd know it anywhere." She made to run towards the boat, but Dad caught her. He made her turn away from the sea, pushing her up the beach.

"He's gone lass, he's gone."

I stood there, cold and wet forgotten, watching them go, Mrs Ruswarp and Mary Jane following slowly with their Sam.

A choking sound behind me made me turn. There was Mam bent double vomiting and Billy clutching frightened to her skirt. I ran to her and was shocked to feel the violent trembling that cut through her body. I couldn't think what else to do but hold her tight and press my hand against her forehead, as she'd done for me when I was sick as a bairn.

The retching stopped, but she still shook. Billy stared white-faced. He'd never seen his strong, quiet mam like this before and nor had I. It had been no easy thing for her to go ploughing out into the sea like that, and of all people I should have known it.

"Come now Mam," I said. "We must get us home."

She nodded and let me lead her back, as though she were a child and I the mam. Billy followed, still holding tight to her skirt.

Just outside our cottage she stopped.

"I'm fine now Liza. I'm myself again. I must look to Irene and we must be thankful that our dad is spared."

"Yes Mam," I said, taking my arm away and letting her and Billy go in first. She was back to being in charge of us all again.

CHAPTER ELEVEN

Dad stayed at home the next night, even though the storm had eased. Our cottage was hushed. Even Billy was quiet, sitting on Dad's knee, watching for Mam's anxious face as she toiled up and down stairs carrying boiling water for Miriam's simples. Our Irene had a fever. Dad sat by the fire all the next day, staring into the grate. He should have been tired, but he couldn't sleep. Grandpa came down to sit with him and they talked in soft voices, saying the same things over and over again.

"I thought I had him," Dad would say. "I threw him a line and he caught it and fastened it. I thought they were safe, but then over they went, with a sudden cutting wave … right sudden, and over went the *Lily Belle*. I hauled young Sam out, no trouble, but I couldn't get hold of John. He was so close, just an arm's length, no more. Just an arm's length and I could have had him."

"Aye," said Grandpa. "It's always the same. You blame yourself when you shouldn't. I've seen more men go down than I can bear to think of and always you say, 'if I'd done this, if I'd done that'. You should not blame yourself. The sea takes those it wants."

"Aye, it does. But it grieves me so that it should take him. Like a son, he was. I taught him all I know and now he's gone, leaving my poor lass like that."

Grandpa spoke very gentle. "He carried the stones you know … so Sam says. Pockets full of dogger, he says. They'd have pulled him straight down. You'd not have got him out… weighted like that."

It made me shudder when I heard that, but I shouldn't have been surprised. There's plenty of the fishermen carry the stones, though it wasn't talked about much. They lived in fear of having a long struggling death if they were thrown overboard, so they didn't learn to swim on purpose – and they carried heavy stones in their pockets so as to make sure they'd sink straight down. Sam Ruswarp is one of the few who can swim well, but I never knew about John.

I hated to think of him with his pockets full of dogger. He must have gone off up the coast deliberate like, looking for the heavy, egg-shaped ironstones that we call dogger, for they're only found where the Cleveland iron seam meets the sea.

Dad shook his head. "He never let on to me. All those times he went out with me and he never let on that he carried the stones. He must have been more feared than I knew."

They'd sit in silence then, Dad stroking Billy's hair, holding him close as though he daren't be letting him go. Then after a while it would all start again. Dad blaming himself and going over all that had happened and Grandpa saying what he could to comfort him.

They'd put Irene in Mam's bed and Miriam was nursing her. I wanted to go up to see her, but Mam said not.

"Soon," she said. "You can see her soon, but leave her to Miriam just now. We must get her to rest real well or … "

"What?" I said. "Or what? What more can happen now?"

Mam bit her lip. "I fear she could lose the bairn. She should not have been out last night, soaked and freezing and pushing at that heavy boat. I couldn't seem to stop her."

"There's nowt could have stopped her, Mam," I said. I sat at our table lonely and useless. I wanted to do something. I wanted to be with Mary Jane, to whisper with her as we did when things went wrong, but this time I couldn't do that for

Mary Jane's brother was drowned and it must be worse for her than me. So I sat on, miserable and sad.

It was late in the afternoon when there came a knock at the door. I opened it to find Mary Jane there with her mother. Mary Jane looked scared.

"It's Mam," she said. "She will not settle, but she must see Irene. I didn't know what to do for the best," and she burst into tears.

I pulled them both inside and Mam came to see what the noise was. Mrs Ruswarp came into the kitchen, calm but determined. "I want to see the lass, that's all. I need to see the lass."

Mam hesitated for a moment, but then she nodded her head. "Of course you must." She led the way upstairs.

I took Mary Jane to sit with me. I put my arms round her and she leaned against my shoulder. We sat there watching Dad and Grandpa, listening to them still, but I felt better after that. I had my job to do, I was looking after Mary Jane.

It was growing dark when Mam came down with Miriam.

"We're leaving those two together," said Miriam. "Best thing for them both, and the fever's less."

"Now, Mary Jane," said Mam. "You must get some sleep. Up into our loft you go with Liza."

We passed Mam's bed on the way up and I went to kiss Irene. Mrs Ruswarp was sitting by the bed, holding her hand ... not talking, just sitting, and Irene was peaceful and resting. I knew then that she would get better, though it might take a long time.

Mam woke us early next morning in her usual brisk way. She sent Mary Jane down to her mother, for Mrs Ruswarp was preparing to return to her cottage.

"What of Irene?" I asked.

"Irene'll do fine," said Mam.

"But what of the … ?"

"The bairn will do fine, so Miriam says, and there's no one better than Miriam for knowing those things. Now, Liza, you're to come with me and fetch the bait."

I stared at Mam. "I'm to go with the flither pickers?"

"Aye, just for today. Irene cannot come and I cannot manage myself, not today."

Mam looked fit to drop. I should have noticed before. She'd have been up in the night looking after Irene, and before that she'd had no sleep for two days and a night.

"I'll go and pick instead of you, Mam."

"Nay, you know nowt about it. Help me for a day or two, but then you must get yourself off to school. Grandpa says he can see to Billy."

"Must Dad go tonight?"

"Aye he must, if the sea allows, for we've still to eat. We must pick for the Ruswarps too, for their Sam's to go with your dad. He must do the same for Sam as he did for John and poor Mrs Ruswarp must steel herself again."

I wrapped myself up warm and laced on Irene's boots. Lad's boots they were. I fastened her quilted petticoat round me, though I had to tie it with string for her stomach had grown so much bigger than mine.

At last I was to go with the bait gatherers. I was to do the work of a proper fisherman's daughter. I clomped down our stairs, curling my toes at each step for Irene's boots slopped a bit. Mam had Irene's bucket and swill ready and a few extra sacks.

"You'll be needing Irene's mittens," she said.

"Nay, I don't need mittens."

We set off down to the scaur, crossing the bridge, for the tide had just turned and it still covered the causeway. Other pickers joined us on the way. There were no greetings or halloos as I knew they usually gave, just a nod or a pat and the unspoken knowing that we must get on with our lives and take from the sea as it takes from us.

Mam put out a bucket and a swill for the Ruswarps and the women dropped their contributions in.

And so I set to work, slipping my blunt knife beneath the limpets to break their hold. The first one took three attempts and I caught my thumb, but soon I thought I'd got the knack. Mussels, the finest bait, went into the swill; limpets, which were more plentiful, into the bucket. I picked away for what seemed a long time, my back bent, for it wasn't worth straightening. I began to ache and straightened then, to ease myself. Mam and the others were hard at it and their buckets half-full.

I went back to work, determined to keep up. I picked and picked, but my knife kept slipping and my fingers gathered cuts that stung with the salt water and the juice that oozed from the shellfish. I found that the best flithers were low down where the tide had been, but that was the wettest, most slippery place.

I stopped again to straighten and rest. Aunt Hannah noticed; she would.

"Why lass, we've nobbut started yet."

Mam brought Irene's mittens from her pocket and handed them to me. I took them quick and grateful, pulling them carefully over my sore fingers.

We picked, it seemed, for hours and hours. I felt as though I'd been out on those slippery rocks trying to fill that bucket all my life. I thought I'd never fill it, though it was

heavy enough to move, as we went further and further away from our village.

I slipped into a shallow pool and cursed at my clumsiness, for I'd soaked my thick petticoat that now chafed cold and wet against my legs. I was soaked anyway, for an angry rain squall drenched us, and still the women picked on.

"I fear we'll be mucking the lines tomorrow," said Hannah. "They'll not be able to get out in this."

"Better to be mucking than having to get the lifeboat out," said Mam.

I could have cried with the weariness of it all. I wondered how we'd ever managed to get the boat out that night. We'd all been soaked and tired then, but we'd not felt it; warmed by fear, we'd been. The flither-picking was quite different. Grim relentless toil, going on and on, and I saw with shame that Mam and even Aunt Hannah were quietly slipping limpets into my bucket as they passed.

I watched Mam's bent back and remembered all the times she'd fought for me to be in school, wanting me to be able to take my chance of something different. I'd have given anything to be in school at that moment.

Still we picked, and I went like one asleep, in a nightmare dream that repeats and repeats, but at last I woke to realise that we were stopping. The women were filling each other's buckets so that we could all return together. They covered the tops with spreading seaweed, for freshness mattered so much.

The walk back was a long weary drag. I was sure my arms were going to break. I kept stopping to rest and getting left behind.

Mam does this every day, I thought, even through most of the freezing winter months. Ahead of me the others reached the causeway and carried their heavy buckets over, making their short cut back to the staithe. Mam turned away and set off up round the bay, her usual long way round. I stopped and put my bucket down. Aunt Hannah had waited for me.

"Now then, look at that," she said pointing. "Just look up there, Liza."

Across the causeway, on the top staithe, was Grandpa, with Billy beside him and a gang of children gathered around him and listening to Grandpa's tales.

"Now that's a sight to make you smile," said Hannah. "It seems there's something good come out of that sad night."

I looked up at the staithe and I wished it were me up there by Grandpa's side.

"But what of Mam?" I said. "I never thought she'd stick to her long walk back, not after she'd gone out so far into the sea that night, pushing the lifeboat through the waves."

"What?" said Hannah. "You thought she'd cross the causeway, did you? Nay Liza Welford, you cannot change a lifetime of fear just like that. Eh, you know nowt lass," and she turned and followed the others, leaving me standing there.

I wanted to follow Aunt Hannah, and get home real quick. I dreaded the thought of the shelling and baiting that was still to be done, but that small shape, steadily plodding away the long way round … drew me. I picked up my bucket again and hurried after Mam, the best I could, shouting her to wait for me.

She stopped, surprised.

"Wait Mam," I shouted. "I want to come your way."

She waited till I came near. "Nay," she said. "You must be daft … but then you don't understand."

"I do, Mam," I said. "I do understand. Gran tried to tell me, but she never got it said. So I asked Aunt Hannah and I asked Miriam, too. I know about your little brother William and I'm right sorry about what happened to him."

She frowned and bit her lip. I wanted to throw my arms about her and tell her how much I loved her, but I couldn't do that. So I did the only thing I could think to do and I wanted it right enough, what with my aching back and cut fingers.

"Mam," I said. "I will go back to school. Not till Irene's better and fit to pick again. But then, I'll go back and I'll work real hard. I will be a pupil teacher, or maybe …" I said, thinking of a thin lady, writing at a desk, with no boots for her feet, "maybe I'll do something else."

Mam's rare slow smile warmed me more than sun.

"That's made me glad," she said.

The Herring Girls

"Bread on the waters! Like manna it was! One hour nothing, the next enough to feed a town, and the sky all lit up with the reflection of the shoal."

Joe Tomlinson – North Sea fisherman

From *Freemen of the Sea*, by Dora Walker, published by A. Brown & Sons Ltd 1951

Dory's Story

CHAPTER ONE

It was late in July; one of those days of sun and heavy showers, worse for us than steady rain. Our mam's the washerwoman and when there's sun we carry the washing up to the lines on Top Green, and when it rains we have to fetch it down again.

I went with Robbie and Alice and we pegged the first lot of clothes and linen out to dry, but even before we got back to our yard, the sky darkened and great spots of rain came pelting down on us. I shook my fist up at the grey clouds and got my eyes splashed full of rain.

"Away back and fetch the clothes in," I said.

We set about the washing, all wet and angry, throwing the clean sheets and petticoats wildly into our baskets.

"Ger'outa my way," I yelled, as Alice reached for the same white sheet as me.

"Great Gawk!" she screamed. "Lanky Dory! You've stuck your elbow in my eye. See what she's done to me, Robbie!"

"Shut up! Daft lasses!" Robbie cried. "You've forgotten Mrs Metcalfe's fine pillowcase, our Dory."

I leapt at the pillowcase, careless of the peg that held it, and as I snatched it down the fine lace edging ripped.

We went quiet then, standing there in the soaking rain.

"Mam'll play war with us," I whispered.

I think we knew then that it would be a bad day.

Mam was bending over the dolly tub, her face and hands

bright red through the steam. She groaned when she saw us coming back, the damp clothes heaped up in our baskets.

"It's all Lanky Dory's fault," Alice cried. "She never turned her boots to Whitby Abbey last night, though I kept on telling her to. She's brought this rain and she's ripped Mrs Metcalfe's best pillowcase too."

Mam pushed the wet hair away from her forehead with the back of her hand.

"Stop it," she snapped. "Stop teasing our Dory so. This rain is none of her fault and if she's ripped a pillowcase, then she shall mend it. We'll just have to grit our teeth and do the best we can. Rob, take the bairns and sit on the step with them. You big girls hang up the linen. We shall have to use the loft, I dare say."

I whispered low to Alice as we climbed up the ladder. "Miss Hindmarch says it's nowt but an old wives' tale, turning your boots towards the abbey to bring us fine weather. It won't do owt, she says."

We spent the whole morning setting up drying lines all over our small cottage and getting crosser than ever. We ended up with a whole day's washing still wet, and in danger of getting itself dirty again. Then at last after midday, the sun came out properly, and we were able to carry some of the washing back up to Top Green.

By late afternoon Mam was still wringing out clothes. Old Mrs Wright had kindly stopped by for a while to turn the handle of the mangle for us, and Alice was lifting petticoats, fresh from the starch tub. The smell of fresh baked bread and fried taties drifted from our neighbours' doorways, but we went hungry.

"Lanky Dory should be doing this," Alice grumbled. "She's biggest and strongest, and my stomach's empty."

I stuck my tongue out at her. She knows how I hate to be called Lanky Dory, just because I'm tall.

"Stop it!" Mam bellowed. She was red in the face, she was that vexed. "Stop that noise, Alice, or you'll feel the flat of my hand." Then she turned to me, and managed to bring a kinder sound to her voice. "Will you run up to the lines again my pet and check if there's owt that's dry? I'll make us a bit of tea for when you get back."

My shoulders drooped at the thought of the hill again, and Alice gave a nasty low laugh as I went to the door.

Though the paving stones and grass were soaking wet, strong sunlight warmed our twisting narrow streets and mist rose everywhere.

I checked the lines, and I found three sheets that were ready for ironing, but then I couldn't face going straight back to our Alice's piping voice and the dank fog of steam that filled our kitchen. I sat down on the edge of the green looking out towards the sea.

I only meant to stay there for a moment or two, but the warm summery wind was fresh on my face. It was peaceful up there, and I could look down onto the busy staithe, and watch the cobles coming back with the tide.

Seagulls swooped down towards the boats, mewing like cats, while the fishermen jumped out into the shallows and splashed thigh deep through the waves, to haul their cobles up onto the shingle.

Our Rob was down there on the staithe with the little ones. I knew what they were after – they'd be begging for fresh boiled crab claws.

A gang of women were gathering on the top staithe, and setting up tin baths and buckets over fires well stacked with driftwood. A cloud of steam rose above them, while the women shouted at the bairns to keep back.

Dan Welford had a good catch of crabs, I could see by the careful way that he lifted the waving claws from the wooden crib of his boat.

I made myself turn away and started to gather in the dry washing, folding it carefully to try to please my mam. I sniffed at it and smiled; it smelt of the sea. Then as I turned to go I glanced back down to the top staithe, and I had to stare again.

Mr Welford and his wife were leaning on the wooden rail and they'd got their six-month-old grandson, Joby, in a fishing basket between them. He peeped over the top like a laughing, wriggling fish. They smiled, but they held themselves quite still. A few yards back from them, a tall man with a beard bent over a wooden box that stood on three thin legs. I knew him at once; we all knew him. He was the Whitby photographer, who tramped about the villages with his camera and his black capes and his folding camera legs. We called him the picture man.

I could see what a fine sight they made, though thick white mist rose from the sea behind them and blotted out the view of the cottages on the far side of the beck.

The picture man waved his arm and pointed, and our Rob went sliding along the rail to sit by Mrs Welford. Their Billy and our young Nan crept up on the other side. I knew that Rob'd be pleased as punch to be put into that picture. They held themselves still as can be for a moment or two, gathered around the laughing baby.

Then all at once the picture was made, and Mr and Mrs Welford were bending down to their baskets to sort out the crabs and lobsters. Our Robbie went to help them as I knew he would. He'd hang around the Welfords for hours, would Rob; anything to do with fishing and you could bet he'd be there in the thick of it.

I started back to our cottage, suddenly sad. I understood our Robbie well enough, for I wished that I was one of the Welfords too; and part of a big busy fishing family.

I wanted it to be my dad, guiding his coble through the sea roads towards Sandwick staithe. I wanted it to be my dad, waving and calling out my name in his deep rumbling voice.

Our mam, Annie Lythe, hasn't always been a washerwoman, and as I'm the eldest I can remember the times when my dad came back from the sea with his lines dripping with cod and ling and haddock.

It was hard work then, for each day we'd have to fix up my dad's lines and fetch the bait, but we used to gossip and laugh with the other families while we worked. Then that terrible spring day came, when the tides were high and the sea was wild and changeable.

Dan Welford had come back at midday, rowing hard against the tide, and the rest of the cobles following, so that everyone ran down to the staithe knowing there must be trouble. They'd seen my dad and his brother Bob with their sail flapping loose and heading dangerously close to Hobs Head rocks. They'd gone to their aid as fast as they could, but our coble had smashed into the rocks and, by the time the Welfords had reached them, there was nowt to be found but splinters of broken mast by the wrecked coble and their flat fishing baskets floating on the water.

Dan Welford has always said that it takes three men to handle a coble and see to the lines. But my dad and his young brother were independent that way. Stubborn was what Mam called it.

Since that day, our mam has kept all six of us from the workhouse by rubbing and scouring at other folks' clothes. The vicar up at Hinderwell raised a bit of money and presented her with a strong iron mangle. So our cottage

is filled with steam and the strong smell of Naptha soap that makes our eyes water. But we don't want to be in the workhouse, nothing could be as bad as that.

We try not to grumble, but we don't like it much. I used to carry fish baskets down to the staithe, not washing to the lines. I'd give anything to go running to help my dad with his catch, and beg a ride up the hill on his shoulders as I used to, twisting my fingers into the stiff salty hairs of his beard.

I sighed as I reached our doorstep. My dad would not know me now for I'd grown too tall to ride on anyone's shoulders.

Though Mam had managed to make us some tea and bread and dripping, she was still very fussed and couldn't listen to the excited chatter of Rob and the bairns, who burst in with tales of being put in a photograph. One of the lines in our yard had snapped, and freshly washed shirts and bloomers had gone down into the mud and must be washed again.

I sighed at the thought of it, but I knew she must be done in.

"Shall I scrub them for you, Mam?"

"Nay, lass," she said, giving my hand a squeeze. "I'm sorry, but you must traipse up to Top Green again, for we've still got Mrs Metcalfe's linen up there, and Alice – you shall have to fetch more water from the spring."

When I got up to Top Green I found the picture man there, crouching beside our washing lines, struggling to get his camera fixed up so that it pointed out to sea across the bay.

He stopped and doffed his hat as soon as I reached the lines. He was like that; treated a fishwife or even a washer-woman as if she were a lady, though he'd always a bit of warmth in his voice.

"Am I in your way?" he asked.

I shook my head, gone all shy.

"I've been watching for that sight all week," he said, his voice deep with pleasure and excitement now. "Here they come … chasing the silver darlings."

I was puzzled for a moment, but then as I looked out to sea, I understood.

Dark sails had appeared on the horizon, heading southerly towards Whitby harbour. Just two or three at first, then quickly the skyline was filled with them. It was the herring fleet, sailing to the fishing grounds where the shoals swim up to the surface at this time of year and they call them silver darlings.

CHAPTER TWO

I smiled, for we look forward each late summer to the coming of the herring fleet. The Whitby fishermen are joined by the Scotch boats, and by others from all along the coast. They even come from Cornwall. Whitby is suddenly bursting with strangers and noise and bustle.

"Won't all that thick white mist spoil your picture?" I asked, forgetting my shyness.

The picture man smiled and shook his head.

"There's many a fine photographer would agree with you, young lady, but not me; I love that mist." Then he sighed. "The boats are moving too fast though, they've a good wind behind them. I should have brought my new box camera that can snap a picture quick as a flash. There's more than twenty boats out there, and I've heard there's more expected. It looks as though there'll be herrings in Whitby tomorrow."

"Aye," I told him. "I went last summer, and I saw it all. I saw the coopers and the dealers and the herring girls. Miss Hindmarch took me."

"Did she now?" He smiled at me with interest. "And what did you think of it?"

"A fine old carry on," I told him.

He laughed. "You're right about that."

Miss Hindmarch is the kindest teacher in our school, and I think she was quite shocked when she found out that I'd never been to Whitby.

"What, Dory? A big girl like you and never been to Whitby?"

"Mam cannot spare me," I whispered, suddenly shamed. The truth was I'd never been further than Hinderwell.

Miss Hindmarch called in at our cottage, and she fixed it up with Mam. She called for me in a pony and trap and took me into Whitby on the next Saturday. It was the best day of my life.

We walked down Flowergate, and I went wild with excitement at the smells and the hubbub of the busy shops. But then I looked out across the harbour to the great abbey high above us on the clifftops and I suddenly stopped. I could do nothing but stare up at those still grey stones, set all about in green, high above the jumbled houses.

Miss Hindmarch asked me what was wrong. I couldn't think what to say to her for I've never been one for clever talk. I blinked and shook my head, then I whispered, "I think that must be heaven up there."

Miss Hindmarch laughed and hugged me. "Have you ever had ice-cream?" she asked.

It was when we walked down towards the pier looking for the ice-cream stall that we saw the herring girls, and what a sight they were; big strong lasses every one of them, standing behind great troughs piled high with silver darlings. Farlanes those troughs were called, Miss Hindmarch told me so. The girls worked like lightning, gutting the fish and slipping them into baskets behind them. Some worked as packers, snatching up the herrings from the baskets, two fish in each hand. They went so fast you couldn't see clearly, or know how they did it.

They shouted, in loud roaring voices, "One pair, two pair, three pair, four…"

"Tally!" another girl bellowed.

Then someone started counting all over again.

The strong-smelling fish guts fouled their oilskin aprons, and spattered their arms. I stared open-mouthed at them, such a wild and frightening lot they were. Miss Hindmarch laughed at my amazement. She shook her head.

"There's no one works like those Scottish girls," she said.

The picture man gave up trying to make a photograph of the fast-moving fleet, and began packing up his camera and boxes.

"That's enough for today," he said. "The light's fading."

I set to helping him, and I lifted his wooden camera legs over the green, looking about for the pony and trap that I'd expected to find.

"How shall you get home?" I asked.

"Why, I shall tramp along to Hinderwell station as I usually do," he told me. "There's the evening train due in half an hour."

"What? And carry all these boxes and things."

"Oh, I expect I shall manage," he smiled.

"I'll help you carry them down the lane," I insisted. The picture man was well known for handing out pennies, and he did not disappoint me, for when I turned back at the end of our lane, he felt deep into his pockets and pulled out three shining pennies and a farthing. I think he'd given me all that was left in his pockets, for he turned them both out and found his return ticket at the bottom.

"Yes, that's all for today."

I thanked him politely and he bowed to me and touched his hat.

"It is a shame that the light has gone or I might have made a photograph of you," he said, looking at me thoughtfully. "Yes, that would be good. A young fisher girl sitting on the bank, watching the herring boats in the distance."

"I fear I'm not really a fisher girl," I said, feeling shy again. "I'm the washerwoman's daughter. You wouldn't want a great lanky lass like me in your picture."

"Lanky?" he said loudly. "Who calls you lanky?"

"My sister does," I whispered, wishing that I'd kept quiet. "All the school children do."

"I'd not call you lanky," he spoke soft now. "I'd call you tall and strong like me. I think it grand to be tall. You can see what others cannot."

I smiled at him then, and waved as he walked on towards Hinderwell, his wooden camera legs swinging from a shoulder strap.

I sat there back on Top Green after the picture man had gone, watching the yellow flickering lights of the herring fleet and thinking of all the gutting that should be done in the morning.

Then suddenly I jumped up trembling and started grabbing dry sheets from the lines. The herring drifters in the distance had lit their riding lights. I'd sat up there staring stupidly out to sea while darkness gathered around me. Mam would go mad.

As I leapt down the steps from the green, my arms full of folded linen, I saw our Alice coming stumbling up the steep pathway.

"Oh, she'll love to see me in deep trouble," I muttered. "I'm coming, I'm coming," I yelled, cursing myself for being so dreamy and daft.

But Alice did not look pleased or gloating. Her face was white and frightened. She burst into tears when she saw me.

"Oh, Dory, I've been shouting and shouting for you. I'm that scared and I don't know what to do. Something terrible has happened to our mam."

I stared at her, my heart thundering in my chest, and my arms so full of piled-up linen that I couldn't run without dropping it.

"Here … take these off me … take 'em quick!"

Alice knuckled the tears from her eyes and held out her arms obediently. Then we both skidded down the steep bank to our cottage as fast as we could.

The stone-flagged floor of our kitchen was awash with soapy water. The big earthenware dolly tub had tipped over and cracked and Mam lay awkwardly beside it on the floor, her hair all soaked in the dirty water. Little Nan crouched in the wet beside her, pulling at her shoulder. Polly stood by the table, staring white-faced at them both.

"Mam's fallen down with a great bang," she sobbed. "She won't get up and she's getting her frock all wet and dirty."

I almost dropped the dry clean clothes I was so scared, but I made myself put them down safely on the table, for nothing vexed Mam more than clean clothes soiled again. Then I ran paddling through the mess to help her.

Mam's eyes rolled and a horrible gurgling sound came from her throat, her mouth slewed over to one side of her face.

"She cannot get up," Alice cried. "I've tried to pull her up, but she cannot."

It was terrible to see my big strong mam, struggling and helpless on the floor like that, and I looked wildly about, wondering where best to get help. Our closest neighbour was Hannah and her husband, Jack, more members of the big Welford family. We call her Aunt Hannah, but then so does half the bay, and Hannah can be very sharp spoken if you're fooling about. But I knew that this was no time to be fearing a telling off, and Hannah would always help when it was really needed.

I ran then and started hammering on her door.

"Hannah, Hannah," I screamed. "Please help us; Mam's took badly."

There was no sound from inside and then I remembered that she'd still be down on the staithe, helping to sort the crabs.

I set off down the bank at full speed, until I met the Welford family slowly carrying up their laden baskets and our Robbie trailing alongside them.

Hannah stopped as soon as she saw me. "What is it, lass?" she asked.

She spoke unusually soft as though she could see at once that I was frightened sick.

"Mam. She's fallen over and cracked our dolly tub."

"Why, never mind, we'll find her another."

"Nay, nay. She cannot get up. She cannot even speak, and her face has… has shrunk to one side and it's horrible."

Hannah thrust her basket into the arms of her daughter, Mary. Then she took hold of me and held my hands tight to make me listen well.

"Now, lass, you must be brave for your mam. Run straight down to Miriam's and bring her quick. I shall go on up to help poor Annie. Come along with me, Robbie, don't look so fearful, lad, we'll see what we can do."

Old Miriam had been midwife, nurse and layer-out to the whole of Sandwick Bay since Mam were a bairn. It was not long before I was puffing back up the narrow cobbled path with Miriam puffing even harder beside me, clutching her basket of herbs and simples.

"Here, carry my medicines, lass," she gasped. "I swear I get too old for this."

CHAPTER THREE

B ut Miriam was not too old for, skinny and bent though she was, she took us in hand and sorted us out before night came. With her help and Hannah's, we got the floor wiped clean and dry and the broken pot taken out to the back. We tucked Mam up in the bed-place downstairs by the kitchen fire.

Martha Welford and her daughter, Liza, brought us a supper of fresh boiled crabmeat and bread and milk. Liza bullied my brothers and sisters up to their beds and settled them all to sleep. She's a clever big girl is Liza and Miss Hindmarch has made her pupil teacher at our school, so we're all well used to doing as Liza Welford tells us.

Miriam patiently fed our mam with spoonfuls of a sleeping draught, and at last she slept, though her face and body still looked all wrong to me. I sat quietly by the fire watching her, while Miriam settled herself in Mam's wooden rocking chair. It seemed she'd be staying the night.

"Miriam," I whispered at last. "Will she die?"

Miriam shook her head firmly.

"Will she mend then?"

Miriam frowned, shaking her head again. "That I can't say. I've seen it before, lass, and sometimes they mend and sometimes they don't."

I sat there in silence staring into the fire and worrying.

"Now, Dory," said Miriam. "Do you remember old Jimmy Loftus who died last spring? Remember how he dragged his left leg just a little bit?"

"Aye?"

"Well, he was same as your mam is now, and he got better fine and lived on for years, and he was a worker, was Jimmy.

You'd never have guessed there'd been anything wrong, just that little drag to the leg gave it away. Nowt to speak of."

"I pray my mam will be like him," I whispered. "Though I hope she will live longer."

Miriam rocked gently in Mam's chair.

"Aye," she nodded. "We'll both pray for that."

I crept up to the loft and climbed into bed beside Alice, and at last I slept. Having Miriam downstairs made me feel safe, despite our trouble.

Next morning I woke quite happy, thinking that it must have been a bad dream, but when I heard Miriam calling up our stairs for me, I knew that it was true and the fright came thundering back. I went down to find a grand breakfast of fried fishcakes waiting for us. Hannah had sent them round.

After we'd eaten, Hannah and Mary came to help us with the bairns, then Miriam told our Rob to take the little ones down to play on the staithe.

"I want to be here to help my mam," Rob said.

"Best way to help her is to give her peace and see to the bairns," Hannah insisted.

Rob sighed, but he did as she asked. I knew he'd rather be doing anything than watching his little brother and sisters.

I could see that all three women were tight-lipped and worried.

"Now we shall have to have a good talk," Miriam said.

"I think Dory should stay," said Mary, putting her arm about my shoulders. "She's a big enough lass and it is her right."

"I want to stay too," said Alice, her thin face all white and drawn.

Miriam nodded and I was glad. I crouched down beside my mam and stroked her hair. Alice came and sat close to me. She pushed her arm through mine, and for once I was really glad of her bony body pressing into my side.

Mam was awake and taking notice of all that went on, though she still could not speak. It was as though all the right side of her body had fallen asleep and would not move or work; not her arm, not her hand, not her leg.

Hannah sat down on the floor to speak to her.

"Annie," she said. "We are going to have to send to Whitby for the doctor."

"Naaah, naaah!" Mam struggled to make them understand.

Miriam bent forwards. "You must be calm, Annie, or you shall make yoursen worse. Tis bad, what's happened to you, and I cannot put you right, but maybe the Whitby doctor can do something. We cannot know unless he come and look at you."

It was then that I whispered aloud the thing that I knew must be troubling Mam.

"We've got no money to pay him with."

"Aye," Miriam sighed. "We shall have to apply to the Guardians. I fear there's no other way."

"But will they not send us to the workhouse?"

Mam lay quiet and helpless beside me, a tear trickled over her cheek.

"Not if we can help it," said Hannah. She bent down and took tight hold of Mam's hand. "I promise you this, Annie Lythe, we shall do all we can to keep you here in Sandwick Bay."

The Doctor came that afternoon in his pony and trap, and we were all sent outside. The little ones ran down to the crab boiling pots, happy enough for the moment, not understanding as Rob and Alice and I did that if the Whitby doctor came to call it must be bad.

We trailed slowly down the bankside after them, and found them greedily poking fresh crab-meat from the claws they'd been given.

Nelly Wright was stirring the boiling tubs, her fat face red and sweating.

"Here y'are, Alice," she shouted, "and you, Dory… tek it then!"

Nelly, who's usually rude to everyone, was trying in her awkward way to be kind to us; thrusting steaming crabs' claws into our faces. I took it, but I'd little stomach for it. I could see sorrow in every face that turned our way. Folk smiled sadly at us, then looked away. It was clear enough; they wondered if we'd be in the workhouse within a week. I couldn't stand their pity.

"Keep your eye on the bairns," I told Alice sharply, and before she'd a chance to complain I was running over the staithe to the beach.

I marched furiously onwards, stamping through the shingle so that it crunched beneath my feet. A warm wind blew straight off the sea into my face, soothing me a little, but still I marched on and on towards the scaur. Then suddenly I stopped; two girls sat together on the big boat-shaped rock that we call Plosher Rock.

Though I wasn't close enough to see them clearly, I knew that it would be Liza Welford and Mary Jane Ruswarp. Best friends they'd always been, and they spent any free moment they had gossiping out there. I walked on, but slowly now, for they sat close together, very still. It was not like them to be so quiet. I almost forgot my own misery as curiosity gripped me.

At last they both turned at the sound of my footsteps in the shingle. I stopped then, ready to turn and run back to the staithe, feeling that I was nosing in on something private.

But Liza grinned and swung her legs round towards me.

"It's all right, Dory. We've got to be getting back. We've just been saying our goodbyes."

I looked from one to the other, wondering who was going where.

I must have looked daft for they both laughed, and jumped down from the rock.

"Did you not know?" said Mary Jane. "This clever Miss Liza is going off to Whitby to play nursemaid for rich visitors for a while."

Liza dug her elbow into Mary Jane's ribs. "She's such a jealous cat. I'm going to have a grand time. I'm to teach the children drawing and look after them, while their family's there on holiday. I'm to have my own room in one of those huge smart houses, up on the West Cliff. Miss Hindmarch recommended me for the place."

"Oh, Liza," I whispered. "A room all to yourself? But Liza," I cried, my own fears crowding back in on me. "I might never see you again."

"'Course you will," Liza laughed, pushing her arm through mine. "I'll be back in the autumn for school."

"But we'll maybe not be here. Miriam says that they must apply to the Board of Guardians to pay Mam's doctor's bill, and I dread that they may send us all off to the Whitby Union Workhouse."

Liza stared at me, then looked over at Mary Jane. "Surely not?"

"Eeh dear, let's hope not," said Mary Jane, pushing her hand through my other arm.

They set off walking slowly back to the staithe, with me between them. I was cheered a bit by their warmth; two big kind girls on either side of me, but they were both quiet.

"I doubt I'll bother going back to school," said Mary Jane. "Now that I'm fourteen I can work with my mam at the bait picking. I can't stay at school just to play on that old organ."

"Take no notice of her! She'll be back at school!" Liza told me cheerfully. "Now that Miss Hindmarch is teaching her to play the hymns, you can't keep her away."

I smiled, for Mary Jane had amazed us all with her playing, and beneath her fingers the old school organ rippled into life.

"I love to hear you play," I told her.

"If there's just one thing I dream about," said Mary Jane, "it'd be to have an organ in my home. I can see it standing there in mam's front room – but they cost so much."

When we reached the staithe, Mary Jane sighed and pulled a face at Liza. "Well, if Liza here is off to be a fine lady, there'll be nowt for me to do in Sandwick Bay. I might as well go off to Whitby myself for the herring gipping."

"What!" Liza exploded.

"Why not? I heard they'd such a good catch yesterday that they were asking for more gutters. Some o' the Scottish lasses have gone to Scarborough this year to suit the dealers."

"You a herring gutter?" Liza laughed. "They'd not have you! Gutting all that fish! It'd kill you!"

"I can gut fish … faster than you."

Liza grinned at her. "But not as fast as the Scottish lasses."

"They get good money," said Mary Jane. "They get as much as a nursemaid. They get more if they're fast, and the catches are good."

"Aye, but look what they have to do for it." Liza shuddered and pinched her nose.

"I thought it was only Scotch lasses that gipped the herrings," I said.

"Oh aye, it's mainly the Scotch lasses. They make it their living, those big tough girls. They manage to do it just about all year round. They start in the spring and get on the trains and off they go wherever the herring fleet takes them."

"But where do they come from?" I asked.

"Oh, from way up north, and they get the trains right down to Lowestoft and Yarmouth in the autumn when the herring shoals swim south. Nobody can work like the Scotch lasses, but then, if the curers are short-handed in Whitby, they'll take on any woman that can do the gutting, just for the season. They'll not have trouble finding them for there's plenty round here that can gut fish. And plenty that want a bit of extra money too."

"Would … would they take me on, d'you think? Maybe I could get some money for my mam?"

"Ey now, Dory," Liza hugged me. "The work they do is terrible. It'll surely not come to that."

CHAPTER FOUR

I walked over the staithe to where Alice and the little ones were playing hopscotch.

"We can take them back now," I told her. "The doctor must have had his say by now. Where's our Rob?"

She nodded her head, looking down to the sea where Rob was splashing through the shallows to help pull Dan Welford's coble up onto the beach.

"Leave him be," I said. "He'll come back when he's ready."

When we got back to Lythe's Yard, the doctor had gone and Miriam was busily whitening our front step.

"Ah, there you are," she looked up from her job. "I'm glad you're back. We've work to do."

"Please Miriam," I begged, "what has the doctor said?"

"Good news, I do believe. The doctor says he thinks your mam will recover in time, but listen well to this," she dropped her voice so that Mam shouldn't hear us. "The doctor says that she must not be vexed or fretful, that could make her worse."

I caught my breath. "But how can she not be fretful when she fears the workhouse so?"

"Aye, it's hard, my pet, I know. But you two lasses can help a great deal by being brave and not fussing. Tomorrow they are sending the Reverend Hawkins down to see us and, as you know, he's on the Board of Guardians."

"Oh no," I cried.

Alice's face crumpled and her chin shook.

"Now, that's what I mean," Miriam told us. "It will fret your mam to hear you weeping. We have to face up to this and all's not lost. Miss Hindmarch has sent to say that she'll come too. She knows the gentleman and she'll do her best to help us. We must get this cottage spick and span so that the Reverend has nowt to complain about, and I shall offer to stay here with you to nurse your mam and see to the bairns. We must beg for just a few outside relief payments, to tide us over the worst."

I nodded my head, seeing the sense of that, though I knew that the Board of Guardians would not willingly give outdoor relief for long.

"Right," said Miriam. "We must set to. There's all this linen to press, then we've to parcel it up and deliver it. Alice, will you run and fetch your Rob? There's errands enough for him to do."

Rob came to help us willingly enough, and he ran up and down our bank with parcels of clean clothes, while we black-leaded our stove and polished it till it gleamed. I tried to tell him what we planned and how we meant to keep us all together with Miriam's help, but he looked miserable.

"Tis the only thing we can hope for," I told him.

"If I had a boat," he said, kicking the heavy iron mangle that stood in the corner of our yard, "then I could be a fisherman, and I could keep us all."

"Maybe one day, Robbie," I said, for I wished the same. "I'd fetch your bait, Robbie, and I'd clean your lines for you, but we've no boat and dreaming won't help us. So leave that mangle be ... I fear we'll be needing it."

Alice and me lay awake that night, curled comfortably together for once.

"Oh, Dory," she whispered. "They say that in the workhouse they make you strip naked and they scrub you down with nasty smelling stuff and they cut off your hair."

"Hush," I tried to soothe her. "Maybe it's not as bad as people say."

"But they make you wear tight scratchy uniforms, I know that's true, for Johnny Liverton's grandpa were born in the workhouse, and he stayed there while he were a bairn. They take the babies from the mams, and they take the lads from the lasses. Oh, Dory, we might never see our Robbie or Jackie again! Would we be put with the twins, do you think? Would you and me be together?"

"Ssh. Don't fret so." I held her tight and stroked her hair. I never knew how much I loved my sister till then. "Hush now," I whispered. "We must not worry our mam."

We were woken next morning by a great knocking on our door. I stumbled sleepily down the loft stairs, wondering why our Rob had not answered the knock. He'd been sent to sleep downstairs in the bed-place now that we'd got Mam settled upstairs.

Miriam came out of Mam's bedroom, yawning and half asleep, in her long white nightgown and sleeping bonnet.

"Are yer there? Are yer up?" A loud voice called, and the knocking continued.

"Whatever's going on?" Miriam sounded quite cross and muddled. "I told young Robbie to wake me soon after dawn."

"I know that voice," I said, running to open the door. "It's Nelly Wright, I'm sure of it."

I'd guessed right. There was Nelly standing on our doorstep, smiling broadly, as though we should be pleased to see her. Almost as though we should be expecting her.

"I've just to let yer know as he's all right," she said. "He'll be back in October with his pay, so he says."

"Let us know what?" Miriam snapped. "Who shall be back?"

"Their young Robbie, of course," said Nelly.

"Where is he?" I asked. "He should be down here, ready to wake us and build up the fire."

Nelly laughed as if that were the greatest joke. "Where is he? He's halfway to Whitby by now. That's what I'm telling yer I passed him on the road an hour since and he'd his pillowcase slung over his back, all stuffed with straw for bedding. He says he's taken half a loaf for his dinner and he's off to Whitby to go with the herring boats."

We just stood there open-mouthed, staring at each other, and then our Alice started to sob.

"Hush," I said, remembering Mam. I clapped my hand over her mouth.

Miriam quickly came to her senses. "Why, you daft lass," she told Nelly. "Why did you not stop him and bring him back?"

"Well," Nelly shrugged her shoulders, puzzled by the fuss. "I thought it were his own business. He's big enough, in't he? How old is he?"

"He's only eleven," I said. "Though he's big for his age, like me."

"They tek 'em at eleven," said Nelly.

"Is that right?" I asked Miriam.

She sighed. "I believe they do, my lass."

"He'll be all right," Nelly told us cheerfully. "And he seems bent on fetching yer some money. Well, I've given yer't message. It's nowt to do wi' me."

And Nelly went off down the street, carrying a heavy pitcher of milk that slopped a little as she swayed.

We stood at our doorway, staring after her. We could think of nothing to say.

Just as we were about to go back inside, a great commotion arose down at the bottom of the bank. It seemed the whole of the Welford family were coming marching up the street. I saw Liza dressed in her Sunday best and then I remembered that she was off to Whitby to be a nursemaid.

"Liza, Liza," I shouted, jumping down from our step and running to catch hold of her arm, "our Rob has taken himself off to Whitby. He says he's going on a herring boat."

"Oh never!" she cried.

"Bless the lad!" Dan Welford cried. "I'm sorry, lass, and I do blame myself. He's been trying hard to get me to take him on with us, for we are going to join in the herringing tonight. I said Robbie should stay here to see to his mam. I ought to have known he'd not take no for an answer."

"It's not your fault, Mr Welford," I said. "You know our Robbie; he'll do nowt he's told."

"We'd all have said the same to him," Miriam agreed. "Will he get taken on, do you think?"

Dan Welford scratched his head. "He might well. The catches are so good that the local boats are joining in. I'll keep a look out for him, young Dory. If he's in any trouble, I'll take him on my boat."

"We'd be much obliged," I said. Then I kissed Liza, and I wished her well.

"I'll see you in October," she told me firmly.

CHAPTER FIVE

The Reverend Hawkins and Miss Hindmarch sat at our kitchen table and sipped tea from Hannah's best china cups. The gentleman was stout with a curling grey moustache. He wore a good black suit, and he'd put down his hat on Mam's rocking chair. Miss Hindmarch nodded smiles at him and us, and complimented Miriam on the cleanliness of the children and of the cottage.

Alice and I stood quietly side by side, our hands linked tightly together. The little ones shuffled impatiently, though I felt proud of the way that they looked; faces and hands scrubbed, their hair brushed smooth and aprons clean. Though Mam was settled in her bed upstairs, I knew she'd be lying awake, straining to catch what was said.

"Do you think perhaps the youngest children could be allowed to go outside now?" Miss Hindmarch asked the Reverend.

He nodded, and Miriam told Alice to take them out. I wanted to go running out with them down to the staithe, running away from all our troubles, but I knew that I had to stay.

There was a knock on the door and Hannah and Martha Welford both came in. They bowed their heads politely to the visitors.

The Reverend Hawkins looked rather surprised. "Relatives only," he said.

Hannah folded her arms and smiled. "Aye. We're all family in Sandwick Bay, sir," she said.

Then our door opened quietly again and in stepped Mrs Ruswarp and old Mrs Wright and, though the clergyman looked puzzled, he didn't object again. After all, what Hannah said was true enough. Though we had no close family left, we had so many second and third cousins that we lost track of who was who.

At last the Reverend gentleman cleared his throat. He turned to Miriam. "What you propose, dear lady, is most generous, and if poor Mrs Lythe were likely to recover her health in a week or two, the Board of Guardians could make such outdoor relief payments. But let us face it, recovery could take months or even years. Mrs Lythe would get proper attention in the hospital wing of the workhouse and the children would be taught their manners and some useful work."

I clenched my hands together behind my back until they hurt, biting my lips to stop the tears from coming.

"I do assure you that they are all good mannered, hardworking children," Miss Hindmarch smiled sweetly at the man. "And they are so close to their mother since their father's death. Might it not seem a great charity to keep the family together?"

"Yes, yes," he nodded impatiently. "But you say the young boy has already gone off to Whitby."

"He's gone off to earn some money for the family," Miriam told the gentleman firmly. "Though we're fearful for him, being only eleven years old."

Reverend Hawkins shrugged his shoulders. "I should say that it's commendable in the child that he's gone to find work. Now, if there were just a little more money coming into the home... some prospect of earnings..."

Suddenly he pointed his finger in my face. "How old are you child?"

I stammered with shock. "I ... I'm thirteen ... sir."

Miss Hindmarch was full of kind concern. "Dorothy's a good girl, but she's never been away from home."

My heart was thumping with fear. I could see the way things were going; I was like to be sent away from home to work. The very thought terrified me, but if it would only keep Mam and the little ones safe here, then I knew I must do it.

"She's tall and she looks strong enough," the Reverend Hawkins insisted. "You say she's helped her mother with the washing. She could be found a place as a laundry maid. Then we might well be in a position to consider outdoor relief payments until her wages are sent home."

There was silence in our cramped little room. The women did not look at me. I knew they would not like the choices being offered, but they could see no other way to help. I must go away and earn us some money, or we'd all be sent to the workhouse. But I was damned if I was going to be a laundry maid.

I had to gather together all the small courage that I'd got and, though my mam was brought so low that she could not speak to me, something that she'd often told me crept into my mind.

"Don't droop your head so, Dory," she'd say. "When you hold up your head and stand tall, there's no finer lass in all the Bay."

So I took a deep breath and I did it. I held up my head and looked straight at Reverend Hawkins, and I said,

"Not a laundry maid, sir. I shall go to be a herring gutter."

Again there was silence and everyone stared at me, but the clergyman smiled, and suddenly he seemed to find me most amusing. I was all muddled in my mind and could only think what strong white teeth he'd got.

"And what makes you think you'll be a herring girl and not a laundry maid?"

I knew the answer to that all right. "My father was a fisherman, sir."

Reverend Hawkins looked amazed, but a ripple of sighs came from the women. They understood.

I smiled. I suddenly knew how to please the man, so I spoke again. "And another thing, sir, a herring girl earns more money if she's fast."

He laughed at that, while the women shuffled and whispered together behind me.

"A herring girl must certainly be fast! Are you fast?"

My usual fear and shyness came flooding back.

"I … I will learn to be, sir."

But Miriam came to stand by me then, snatching up my hand in hers. I think she knew that my courage had ebbed away as fast as it came.

"'Tis terrible hard work for a little lass, but if Dorothy feels that she can do it, then I can certainly see to the bairns and nurse her mother while she's away."

Miss Hindmarch looked worried at the way things were going, but the vicar turned to her shaking his head.

"It's quite ridiculous! Good-mannered did you say? The girl must be a laundry maid. It's what she's been taught."

My heart sank heavy as ironstone.

But then Hannah came to stand on the other side of me.

"The girl can gut fish," she said. "I've taught her that. You said yourself, sir, she's tall and strong."

"So I did, but, well, don't those women work in teams?"

"Aye, they do. But we shall find a team from the village. We can fix her up as one of three."

The Reverend Hawkins face grew serious. "Doesn't she need equipment, knives and such like?"

"We'll find her the knives and mittens and apron, sir." It was Martha Welford speaking now.

The man looked up at the women. Something had changed in our small kitchen. They'd gathered around me like a warm, strong blanket. They spoke as one, with stubborn determination. I'd seen it before, often enough. They'd gang up on a man who beat his wife, or strip the trousers from a lad who courted too freely. I could not believe it, for though they must think I'd gone barmy, still they stood by me.

Hannah spoke for them all.

"If the child can face the hard work, then we shall find her all she needs."

It wasn't till the visitors had gone that it really hit me, as I came to realise what I'd let myself in for. I started shaking all over so that Miriam made me sit by the fire and sip some hot sweet tea.

The women didn't fuss me.

"Aye, she's bound to feel like that," said Hannah, in her matter-of-fact way. "You can sit for a bit, Dory, but you can't sit for long; there's much to do. I shall go straight down to the staithe to speak to our Jack. He and Dan are making the plosher ready for the herringing."

"Right," said Martha. "We'll see if they'll hold back a hundred herrings, for we'll have to teach her to gip."

"But I can gut a haddock or a cod," I said, quite offended. "Didn't Aunt Hannah tell the gentleman that I could?"

"Never mind what I told him!" said Hannah. "Gipping a herring is quite a different matter, and I shall have told no lie, for I will teach you to gip before you go to Whitby, and you are going to have to learn fast, my girl."

"We'll send a message to Cousin Rachel," said Martha. "She sometimes lets her rooms to herring girls. She used to be fond of Annie, when we were lasses. She'd help you out, Dory, and keep a bit of an eye on you too."

"That's a grand idea," Hannah agreed. "But first things first. Finding a team of three is the sticky thing. 'Twould be best if we could find someone who's done it before. Your Irene would be good, but I doubt if she'd leave that bairn."

Martha shook her head. "I'd have the little lad, quick as a flash, she knows that, but she's besotted with the bairn."

I got up from the fireside, for I'd my own ideas about who might make up the team, and I knew I must get busy before I got too scared and changed my mind.

"I think I might know someone who'd go wi' me."

"Our Nelly might," said old Mrs Wright as she set off home. "She were on about it the other night. I'll speak to her."

I said nothing till she and Mrs Ruswarp had gone, but I wasn't keen on going off to Whitby with their Nelly. Miriam's sharp eyes caught the look on my face.

"You could do worse than Nelly," she told me. "I seem to recall that Nelly's done the gipping before, and again it were illness that caused it. Her father was laid up one summer with a bad leg, and old Mrs Wright took Nelly off to Whitby with her. They worked all through the season, and Nelly can't have been older than you are now, Dory. She's a tough 'un, is that Nelly, and that's who you want gipping beside you… a tough 'un."

CHAPTER SIX

I scooted down the bank as fast as I could, looking for Mary Jane, my whole body prickling with the excitement of it all. I hadn't said anything to Mrs Ruswarp about it for I didn't know what she'd think, Mary Jane being her youngest

Alice was sitting on the staithe with our twins and Jackie. I knew I must tell her and not waste time.

"Well?" she cried. "What have they said?"

"We're not to go in the workhouse so you can stop worrying about that. I'm to go off to Whitby to gip the herrings and earn us some money."

"Oh no, Dory, no. You cannot do that. Not you and Robbie both gone."

"Now stop that," I wagged a finger in her face. "I'll be back when the herrings move south in October, and Miriam will look after you till then."

"I don't like Miriam," she said, her chin trembling. "She's old and snappy."

I sighed and I put my arms about her. "Come on, Alice. You've to be the big lass now."

"I'm our big boy," little Jackie spoke up cheerfully, catching what we said. "I'm our big boy now Robbie's gone."

"Aye," I said, and I reached out and slapped his rump to tease him. "You're the big boy. Tell our Alice that she must be the big girl."

"Big girl," he said giggling, and thumped Alice on the head.

"Big girl, big girl," the twins echoed.

I turned serious, "It's either Miriam or the workhouse. Which do you want Alice?"

A faint smile touched her lips. "If that's what I've got to choose, then I want Miriam," she whispered.

There was no sign of Mary Jane on the staithe or in the yards, and I was just wondering whether I'd have to go knocking on the Ruswarps' door when it came flooding into my mind that I knew exactly where she'd be.

I ran across the staithe and onto the sand. It was a hot afternoon, and the rocking of the waves sent glittering shots of sunlight into my eyes. I was dizzy with the regular swish and fizz of the sea, as it washed against the pebbles. The faster I tried to go, the more my feet seemed to sink into the soft dry sand. But Mary Jane was there, just where I thought she'd be; a lonely figure sitting on Plosher Rock.

"Mary Jane! Mary Jane!" I yelled at her, waving my arms.

She looked up at once and stared at me, then she turned away disappointed. I swear she'd hoped for a moment that it was Liza Welford, come back to Sandwick Bay. I could see that she didn't feel much like bothering with me, but I'd no time for messing about.

"Please Mary Jane," I panted, crunching through the shingle, and throwing my arms over Plosher Rock. "Please Mary Jane, I'm begging you. Will you come with me to Whitby to gip the herrings?"

"What?" she stared at me amazed.

"Well, I am surely going," I told her. "It's all fixed. I've either to do that or go as a laundry maid, and I'd rather be a herring gutter. The Guardians will make outdoor relief payments for my mam if I go away to earn some money. So you see I've got to go, but now I must find myself two more to make a team of three, and fat Nelly might be one of them – but I hope not."

The words tumbled fast from my mouth; I couldn't stop to draw breath.

Mary Jane listened to it all in shocked silence.

"You must be mad," she said at last.

I waited by the rock, dismayed and miserable. I knew that I could not wait for long. If she would not come with me, I must get on and find another.

"Well," I said at last. "I thought I'd ask, after what you said yesterday. I daresay you were only teasing Liza, and never meant it. You've no desperate need to earn money, not like me."

I turned to go, and started back across the shingle.

"Wait!" Mary Jane called after me. She swung herself down from the rock, and ran to push her arm through mine. "Wait a while. I do want money! I *was* only teasing yesterday, but now you've made me think. Could I earn enough to buy an organ?"

I smiled. "If the catches are good, and we can work fast enough, then I think you might."

"I'll be miserable here in Sandwick without Liza, and now you're going too, Dory. At least it's all go in Whitby, though I swear the work will kill us."

"I daren't even think about it," I told her. "I've just got to go and do it."

"Well," said Mary Jane. "We'd better find another to make up our team, and not Nelly Wright."

"You'll come then?"

"I must be mad! But I'll come with you. I'd best go to tell my mam."

Mrs Ruswarp frowned at us both, and then she sighed, but she accepted it.

"You seem such little lasses to be going off to work like this. Still, I know that you must go Dory lass, and most folk would think that Mary Jane is quite old enough at fourteen. It's just that she's my baby, you see."

Mary Jane kissed her mam. "Wait till you see the money I'll fetch back wi' me. And Mam, how would you like to see a beautiful polished wooden organ standing in your parlour?

Mrs Ruswarp smiled and shook her head. "Just see that you find an older body for the third."

We went knocking on the Welfords' door to see Irene. We didn't hold out much hope of her coming, but we thought she'd be the best one to ask; her being kind, and having done the gutting before.

"I thought she'd maybe need a bit of money for the bairn," I whispered to Mary Jane, but she shook her head.

"You know their Frank? The one that went fighting in the war! Well, he's got himself a job up at Stockton now, working in the steelworks. He sends Irene money every week or so, to help her with the baby. Our John were his best friend you know."

I nodded silently, sorry that I'd reminded Mary Jane of her poor drowned brother John.

Irene opened the door with little Joby in her arms.

"I know what it is that you want, Dory, but this bairn's right fretful and awake all night. He's starting cutting his teeth as well, so that I can't bear to leave him with my mam."

Joby smiled at us, and dribbled.

"Give your auntie a kiss," Mary Jane insisted, smacking her lips at Joby till he giggled.

Everyone in our village treasured the baby boy, for none of them could ever forget the fierce storm that had drowned his father, and the terrible struggle that they'd had to save the other men.

Irene had had a hard time getting through her pregnancy, she'd been so sick and so miserable. But then when Joby was born, she'd not stayed sad for long, for you'd never seen a bairn with a happier, funnier face. Just one look at him and you had to smile, whether you wished to or not. Irene had named him John, for his father, but the villagers had insisted on calling him John's boy, and after a while it had shortened itself to Joby.

"I don't blame you for not wanting to leave him," I told Irene. "I'd not want to leave him either. Mary Jane is going to come with me."

"Eeh dear! I hope you both know what you're taking on," she said. "I've got something for you, though. I've gipping knives and a good wooden trunk. Come on in and have a look!"

The trunk was a proper kist box, the kind that the Scotch girls used, with its wooden shottle drawer at the top, made specially to hold the knives, and space beneath for clothes.

"I'd think you two could share one box," said Irene. "It's not as though you're going right down to Yarmouth, like the Scotch girls do."

I agreed with that for the trunk looked big to me, and I'd nothing to put in it. I'd only my best clothes and my working clothes and that was it.

We carried the kist box round to the Ruswarps' cottage, and then we went banging on the Pickerings' door.

Bessie Pickering was one of the younger married women who'd got no children. She smiled when she saw us and asked us in. It seemed the whole village knew our business.

"I do wish you well," she said. "I was meaning to help with the gipping this year, but I've just come to realise that I'm expecting. I've wanted a bairn for more than three years now, so I'll not take any risks with it."

We said that we were pleased for her, and we were just about to go when she lifted a great pile of cotton strips down from her sideboard.

"I've been saving flour bags all through the winter," she said. "I've cut them into bandage strips. You'll be needing these now, instead of me."

I remembered then how the herring girls must bandage up their thumbs and their first two fingers to save them from the cuts. We took the cotton strips most gratefully.

Though we knocked on doors all through the afternoon, we could not find a woman who was willing and free to come gipping with us. Still, we didn't come away empty handed. We were given strong oilskin aprons, with straps that crossed at the back, old working skirts and shirts, and worn-out knitted ganseys. There was a pot of Mrs Love's ointment for curing cuts, and a deal of sound advice to go with it.

Mary Jane and I were worn out when we got back to the Ruswarps' cottage, our arms piled high with gifts.

"Mam! You should see what we've been given," Mary Jane called out. "But we've still got nobody to make a third."

Mrs Ruswarp nodded her head towards their kitchen. There standing in front of their fire range was Nelly Wright.

"Yer should have asked me," Nelly said. "I'll come to Whitby wi' yer. There y'are then … that's all right."

CHAPTER SEVEN

It was quiet back at the cottage. Miriam had sent the three younger children off to bed and she and Alice were ironing our Sunday-best clothes. Buckets of washing were soaking out in the yard.

"More washing?" I said. I wanted to cry when I saw those buckets. "They'll keep on sending it, won't they? What shall we do? And why have you ironed our Sunday clothes?"

Miriam smiled and shook her head. "Don't you always press your clothes on Saturday night?"

"It can't be Saturday already," I said.

So much had happened that I'd got my days all muddled.

"Stop fussing, Dory," said Alice, suddenly all grown-up. "This is our washing. We've not had much chance to deal with it, so we've set it to soak till Monday. Miriam has sent messages telling our customers that Mam is sick and cannot take in washing for a while."

"Oh thank you, Miriam," I said, relieved. Suddenly I was blinking back tears. "You're doing that much to help us and I can't see as we can ever repay it."

Miriam waved her hands in the air. "Now Dory, you know that I never had bairns of my own so I'm glad o' the chance to see to other folks little 'uns."

I nodded my head and wiped my eyes.

"Mam's wanting you," Alice told me. "She's made it plain enough."

"What shall I say to her?" I looked at Miriam.

"Say nowt," Miriam shrugged her shoulders. "I've told her that you're off to Whitby. I don't think she likes it much, but she can still think straight; she knows there's little choice. Now up you go, she wants to see you."

Mam was propped up on the pillows. Miriam had left an oil lamp burning low on the small cupboard beside her, so that Mam's silver hairs glowed golden against the brown ones. She looked a bit better to me.

"Oh, Mam," I said, and I went to put my arms about her. We stayed like that for a moment my cheek against hers; she stroked my hair with her good hand. But then she pulled away.

"What is it?" I asked.

"Naah … naah!" Mam pointed down towards the bottom of the bed.

"What is it you want?" I asked stupidly. "A rug? A drink? Miriam?"

"Naah … naah." She tried again, and I carefully followed where she pointed.

"Dad's sea chest?"

She nodded at last, and beckoned me to bring it to her.

I grabbed the handle of the heavy chest and dragged it across the room. I lifted the lid with shaking hands. Most times Mam would not let us touch it, though we knew well what was inside. We treated those few poor things with reverence: Dad's old clothes, his Sunday-best suit, his three clay pipes all different sizes and his bowler hat.

Mam lurched to the side of the bed, trying to reach down into the trunk.

"What is it?" I asked again.

Mam couldn't seem to find what she wanted. She waved her good hand wildly in the air.

"Naah! Naah," she cried out with rage. I was feared to see her so vexed and helpless.

"Whatever is wrong?" Miriam appeared at the top of our narrow stairs.

"I do believe she wants me to tip Dad's sea chest out."

"Well, in that case, I should do it, lass."

So I did, I tipped all my father's things so that they rolled out onto the bedroom floor. Mam calmed down straight away; she went quiet and thoughtful, inspecting the stuff carefully, then at last she pointed clearly at his boots.

"Dad's sea boots?"

Mam nodded, and I picked them up. They were his best pair and they were almost unworn.

"What am I to do with them?" I looked at Miriam, puzzled.

"You're to wear them, Dory, what do y'think?" Miriam chuckled and Mam pointed to my feet

"I'm to wear my dad's best boots?" I whispered.

"I think your mam wants that," said Miriam. "There's nowt better for a herring gutter than sea-boots. You've to stand for hours in the muck and wet, and they'll keep you comfortable and dry. There's many a herring girl wears her dad's old boots. You're to have a strong decent pair that's hardly worn."

I shook my head. "They're too big."

It wasn't really the size that troubled me, more that it seemed a sinful thing to wear my poor dead father's boots.

"They won't be," Miriam said firmly. "Not when you've three pair o' woolly socks inside 'em."

I looked at Mam, and I could see that she tried to smile though it came out all lopsided. A tear ran down her cheek.

"Oh thank you, Mam," I said, hugging the boots to my chest. "I'll take good care o' them and clean them well when we're finished. Now I've got summat precious to put in Irene's kist."

Miriam made us go to Sunday school, as we usually did, and I sat quietly beside Mam's bed all Sunday afternoon.

On Monday I woke early and I dressed and went straight round to Hannah's cottage, for Hannah had promised to teach us how to gip herrings. Mary Jane was there, looking sleepy and yawning.

"Is Nelly learning to gip?" I asked.

"She is not." Mary Jane giggled. "Fastest herring gipper in Sandwick is Nelly ... or so she says."

We'd got three baskets with two hundred over-day herrings that Jack and Dan Welford had kept back from the dealers on Saturday, so that we could practice our gipping. It was good of them, for decent-sized herrings were selling for three shilling a hundred in Whitby.

"They've landed six lasts in Whitby this week," said Hannah.

We were impressed at that, for it meant more than sixty thousand herrings caught in just a few days' work.

"And they're expecting more Cornishmen to arrive tonight. It's just like the old days. Fancy them Cornishmen sticking to fishing out of Whitby, when so many dealers have gone over to Scarborough."

"Why is Scarborough so favoured?" I asked.

"The dealers are asking for new building work to be done on Whitby harbour, but the Board hasn't got the money to do it." Hannah shrugged her shoulders. "So it's loyal of these Cornish chaps to stick with us. Our Jack says Whitby's the place for Penzancemen, no matter what. They like the chapels, see."

"Has Mr Welford seen owt of our Robbie?" I begged.

Hannah shook her head. "I'm sorry, lass, but they'll be looking again today, and you must seek for him yourself when you get there. I've asked our Jack and Dan to take you lasses round to Whitby tonight?"

"What?" said Mary Jane. "We've not even learnt how to gut a herring yet!"

"You'll have learnt by tonight or never," said Hannah. "They're telling me the curers have fixed up three teams of Whitby women. Either you go tonight or you'll have missed your chance. Our cousin, Rachel Welford, has sent to say that she's getting her downstairs room ready for you. She'll see you're all right."

Mary Jane pulled a face, and whispered in my ear. "Aye. She'll see us all right. Just like Hannah, she is."

"What's that?" said Hannah. "No time for fooling, Mary Jane, you fetch those gipping knives and the oilie aprons. We must get on."

"Oilie aprons? While we're just learning?" Mary Jane looked amazed.

"Aye … you'll put on aprons, boots and bandages. You're like to make a worse mess now than ever, and you don't want to start it all with a bad cut. Come on! Fetch all the stuff! Spread that oilskin on my table top!"

Hannah made us bandage up our fingers carefully, and tie the knots with our teeth for, as she said, there'd be nobody to help us in Whitby, and no time to help each other. I knew then what a grand present Bessie had made us, for we'd never have been able to find the stuff and carefully cut up all those bandages ourselves.

My first attempts at gipping were useless.

"Nay, Dory, lass," Hannah cried. "You're bringing out good flesh. Here let me stand behind you. Start slow and get it right! You'll come into speed later.

I gripped the plump silver-skinned fish and Hannah put her hand over mine to guide the short sharp gipping knife.

"There now, make the cut in its throat like that, then push

130

in so. Now a quick twist to pick up the guts, then gently flick – and out they come."

The strong-smelling herring guts slopped out onto the oilskin cover.

"Is that it?" I asked. The fish stared mournfully up at me, its eyes still bright on either side of its upturned nose. It looked almost untouched, just a small neat hole in its throat.

"That's it," said Hannah. "So long as the gut and the gills are out. Now try yourself."

I copied her carefully, trying to judge the right spot to push in my knife, and just the right angle to pick up the guts when I twisted. And I did judge it right, but I pulled the knife out far too fast and a slimy spurt of fish guts shot up into my face. The stinking guts went up my nose, and into my mouth.

Hannah snorted with laughter and Mary Jane shrieked out loud. I staggered back, spluttering and spitting. The herring guts tasted foul.

"Ugh! Dory," yelled Mary Jane.

"Eeeh! Dory love," cried Hannah. "I know it's wicked to laugh. But … oh, your face! The guts should go in the gut tub, ma bairn! There's a cloth behind you. Now then, come on, we'll try again."

I wiped my face and shuddered, I couldn't stop spitting.

"It's all right you laughing," I told Mary Jane. "I've not seen you bring the guts out yet."

We worked slowly all morning under Hannah's instruction, and when we'd used up almost thirty herrings, we'd begun to get the knack of hitting the right spot and bringing the guts out each time. Our arms and aprons were spattered with mess and our bandaged fingers slippery and wet, but Hannah had made us work slowly and we'd not cut ourselves.

Hannah set three baskets behind us and showed us how to judge the size of each herring, and throw the gutted fish carefully into the right basket. The smallest ones were called Matties. The medium-sized fish were called Mattiefulls, and the largest herrings were called Fulls. Hannah made us guess the size and shout it out as we gutted. If we guessed wrong, she scooped the fish out and made us do it again. At noon she let us stop.

"I'll make us a pot of tea," she said. "Though there'll be no stopping for breaks in Whitby you know."

Mary Jane slumped down onto a chair.

"Mind my decent furniture with those filthy oilies!" Hannah snapped. "You can sit on the doorstep if you must."

We sat on Hannah's doorstep and sipped our tea. Apart from the gentle babble of Alice and the bairns next door, the village seemed deserted. I frowned. Where had they all gone? Then suddenly it came to me.

"Is it Regatta Day?" I asked.

"Why, you great daft head," Mary Jane laughed. "O' course it's Regatta Day. You must be flummoxed with all your troubles, Dory."

I nodded, and I turned to Hannah, who'd stood on her doorstep hands on her hips. "You've missed Whitby Regatta to teach us how to gip."

Hannah smiled kindly and shook her head.

"I've seen plenty of regattas, ma lass, and I daresay I'll see plenty more."

Mary Jane groaned, and rolled her shoulders back.

"I'm aching already," she said. "We must be mad! Why are we doing it?"

"Money," I answered her quickly. "Think of that fine organ standing in your mam's best room."

I didn't need to remind myself how badly that money was needed for us.

CHAPTER EIGHT

The two Welford brothers had to row hard for the tide was against them. I clutched tight to the side of their plosher that was named the *Esther Welford*. She was one of the big five-man coble boats that the Whitby men use for chasing the herring. They'd come away from the regatta early, in order to fetch us back to Whitby before the herring fleet went off for the night.

The afternoon had passed in a whirl of fast fish gutting, cleaning us down, and then frantic last minute packing of Irene's trunk.

I was all of a dither, and I think Mary Jane was worn out and regretting her promise to come to Whitby and work with me. Nelly had come up to Hannah's to watch us gip.

"Yer'll have t'work faster 'n that," she told us. "Ey dear, I can see as I'm going to be having to do most of t' gipping. You two'll have to take turns at packing."

"I shouldn't think they'll complain at that," Hannah said.

"You don't have to come with us, Nelly," Mary Jane said, hopefully.

"I'll put up wi'yer," said Nelly. "I've got me box ready now."

We'd been so busy that I couldn't think straight. I hadn't said a proper goodbye to my mam or to Alice. It was Miriam who came down to the staithe to see me off. Our Jackie and little Nan and Polly came with her, waving at me, all cheerful and excited. I don't think they realised that they'd not be seeing me again for two months. They thought I was just having a nice ride out in the Welfords' plosher.

Nelly sat beside me, smiling calmly as the big coble pulled out of the bay, taking it all in her stride. She was twenty and one of the few older lasses who'd no young man to court her. I'd always been wary of her; for she'd tease the bairns and she could be right rough and loud-mouthed. You never quite knew what she'd do or what she'd say.

Mary Jane sat in the stern along with her brother, Sam, who often worked the boat with the Welford brothers. She was telling him that she'd have finished his gansey by the time the herring season was over.

"You ought to knit a gansey, Dory," she told me. "All the herring lasses knit ganseys and sometimes we'll be waiting around for the boats to come in."

Knitting the warm jumpers that we call ganseys is vital work for all fishermans' wives and daughters. There's never an excuse for idle hands in our small village and the women are knitting away every spare minute of the day. Without their ganseys to keep out the wet and cold, our men would freeze out on the sea.

I shrugged my shoulders. "Who should I knit for?" I asked.

"Your Robbie of course; he's a fisherman now, in't he?"

"Aye, maybe," I answered. "But if I find him safe, I'll send him home."

Nelly laughed and shook her head. "He'll not go," she told me. "He'll not tek notice of his sister fussing at 'im. Not that lad. He were that determined when he spoke to me."

I sighed. "If he'll not go home, then I'll start to knit him a gansey," I said.

We fell quiet as we left our bay. My stomach lurched as the boat rolled with the waves. In the distance, we could see the fleet of visiting herring boats riding at anchor in the sea roads off Whitby harbour.

I smiled to myself. I remembered the delicious smell of fried herrings that had come to us as we carried our boxes down to the staithe. We'd laughed about it. The smell seemed to waft from every window and every doorway. The whole of Sandwick Bay had come back from Whitby Regatta, full of excitement at who'd won the coble race and who'd won the long boat race, to find they'd cheap fresh herrings, some rather roughly gipped, for their tea. Hannah had sent our Jackie and Billy Welford round the houses selling the herrings that we'd gutted at a halfpenny a pair.

The sea grew choppy, and the sky darkened as though we might be in for rain.

"We're going a long way out," I said, trying not to sound worried.

I'd not had much chance to go out in the boats since Dad died.

"Don't fret, young Dory," Dan Welford winked at me. "We have to follow the sea roads, so we don't catch the scaur. They're right awkward are those low-lying rocks. They stretch for more than a mile, so we must go out a bit further at times, just to keep ourselves clear of them."

"I'd not want to do this every day," I said. "Our Robbie must be daft.

"Aye, we're all daft," Jack Welford said cheerfully. "And your Robbie's a stubborn fellow, just like his father was."

There were spots of rain and the boat rocked wildly as we drew close to the Cornish boats with their double masts and lug sails. I was feeling very sick, and wondering what the men'd say if I begged them to take me back to the bay, when they turned the boat southerly to ride with the tide and we could see Whitby harbour small and flat looking and misty in the distance.

We went towards it fast then; my stomach pulling itself tight with excitement. My spirits lifted with the boat as it rode the waves towards the town.

As soon as we passed through the curved arms of the harbour, the sea grew calm, and Whitby Town seemed to rear itself about us on either side of the river Esk.

Smoke from the chimneys mingled with the mist.

"Oh, look at the Abbey," I shrieked at Mary Jane. "And St Mary's church up on the clifftop, and all those grey stone stairs."

"Henrietta Street," she shouted, pointing wildly at the old street that ran below St Mary's church. The small houses up there seemed lost in clouds of puthering smoke. "See, it's got the little beach below it. That's where we're stopping."

"I don't know what yer both yelling about," said Nelly. "This here's the fish quay where yer'll be working. And yer'd better get used to the smell of bloaters and red herrings, for Henrietta Street's nowt but smoke-houses these days."

Hannah's Cousin Rachel was waiting for us by the fish quay on Pier Road. There were no herring girls in their usual places that day as all the work had stopped for the regatta. Rachel was a small woman, about Mam's age, with grey hair combed smooth beneath the cotton headscarf that many of the fisherwomen wore in the summer months. She stood by the harbour rail, her arms folded over the top of a spotless white apron. She had that stony, determined look that I knew well. Most of the fishwives had that same look. You'd have a job to pull the wool over their eyes.

She gave Mary Jane a quick kiss and turned to me.

"Now then honey, so you're Annie Lythe's oldest lass. I knew your mam when we were young. You've more a look of your father though. Now then, Nelly! I spoke to the curer's chaps this morning and told them you were on your way, but they've fixed up two more teams and they say they don't need any more at the moment."

"You mean we're too late?" Mary Jane looked horrified.

I couldn't bear the thought of going back to Sandwick Bay empty-handed now that we were here in Whitby.

"Can we not ask again?" I tried to make my voice sound calm, though I was desperate inside.

"'Course we can," Nelly told me. "Yer can't expect to be taken on just like that."

"Oh aye. We must ask again tomorrow," Rachel said kindly. "No need to give up yet, hon. I've heard all about your mam, and I know you need the work. The room's all cleared and ready for you, so come on back to Henrietta Street and I'll make you a bit of tea."

We said our goodbyes to Dan and Jack, but I kept staring at the big wooden farlanes that the coopers were setting up on Pier Road, ready for the herring girls in the morning.

"Come on," Nelly said. "Never mind gawping at them, time for that tomorrow. Tek up my box, wi' me will yer! Rachel and Mary Jane have taken yours."

I took the nearest handle of her box and helped carry it.

"Can yer not hold it up a bit," Nelly complained as we followed the others over the bridge.

I'd remembered that I should be looking out for our Robbie, and what with that and the busy streets my head turned this way and that. We went down Sandgate, and up through the market place, and along Church Street. It was full of the whirring of machines and tapping sounds that came from the busy jet workshops.

"They're doing all right here, they are," Rachel told us. "Ever since the old Queen lost her husband and took to wearing the black jet stones in her jewelry, business has been booming."

We reached the bottom of Abbey stairs and went past them into Henrietta Street.

"Eeh, you can smell bloaters up here." I laughed, my eyes watering a little.

"You'll soon get used to it," Rachel said. "Mr Fortune's sheds are up on the bankside, just opposite my bedroom window. I'm so used to it, I only ever take notice if he's *not* got fish smoking for some reason."

Nelly's box was heavy and I was ready to drop it when Rachel stopped to open her front door. It was one of the last few cottages on the harbour side of the street, though the pathway carried on past more smoke-houses and led down to the East Pier.

The door next to Rachel's opened and a woman stuck her head out; another fisherman's wife, by her bonnet and apron. She looked at our boxes, surprised.

"Now Rachel, what's this? I thought you weren't taking Scotch lasses this year."

"I'm not," said Rachel. "This lot's from Sandwick. You've seen Mary Jane before, and this is Annie Lythe's lass, Dory, and Nelly Wright you know."

"Have they fixed them up, then?"

"No," said Rachel. "They'll have to try again in the morning."

The woman clicked her tongue and shut her door.

"That's my neighbour, Hannah Smith," Rachel told me. "She's known as Trickey round here. You can guess why! She's a good enough neighbour to me though. She's got eight of the Scotch lasses stopping with her. You'll hear them when they come back."

I stared at Trickey's door. Eight Scotch lasses! Where did she put them all? The cottages were bigger than ours in Sandwick, but they weren't that big.

Rachel went into a narrow passage with a door to the right. She flung it open, and we saw a small bare basement room with three steps down to it.

"There you are," Rachel said. "I've put you in here, so you don't need to traipse through the rest of the house."

Nelly and I followed the others in, bumping her box down the three steps.

The room was so dark and dismal that my spirits sank. It was all so very bare, nothing in but three beds, covered with worn patchwork quilts. Our living rooms at Sandwick bloomed with fine brass ornaments and pictures and somehow I'd expected the same. In Rachel's room the floorboards were covered with oilcloth, and the curtains that hung at the window, just above the street level, had brown paper pinned carefully over them. There were no curtains at all on the far small window that overlooked the harbour and beach.

"I've had a good clear-out, as you can see," Rachel told us, as though we should be pleased. "So now you won't need to worry about the mess."

"Aye," said Nelly. "I prefer it like this," and she thumped herself down on the bed nearest to the street window.

"I'll make some tea, and give you a shout," said Rachel. "You can come up to my kitchen today, but once you're working I'll bring your food and drink down here to you. I'll want your boots and oilies left outside of course."

The three of us were left together. Nelly swung her legs up onto her bed, trying it and prodding it.

"Not bad," she decided.

Mary Jane looked across at me. I think she felt a bit lost too.

"I knew they cleared the best furniture out," she said. "I just didn't think how plain it'd leave it. We haven't even a chair to sit on."

"We sit on't boxes, of course!" Nelly said, disgusted at our ignorance.

I went to peep out of the window on the harbour side, and I got a grand view of the West Cliff and the boats in the harbour, making ready to set off for the night.

"Can I have this bed?" I asked, going to the nearest one.

"You can," said Nelly. "I'm not sleeping there. I don't want the sea keeping me awake all night."

CHAPTER NINE

Rachel called us up to her kitchen and I was glad to see that it was as bright and cosy as any in Sandwick Bay. She served thick slices of bread with a little butter and sweet bilberry jam.

"The bairns fetch t' berries down from the moors," she told us. "Then they come round knocking on doors with their hands and faces stained black and purple. They've the cheek to ask a penny a basket, but they're fine berries for jam, and my husband has a sweet tooth, so I usually buy from them."

The food cheered me for a moment. It looked as though we'd be well fed if nothing else. Then a terrible thought came to me and I had to put down my bread and jam.

"Oh dear," I cried, going red with the shame of it. "If the curers won't take us on, we'll get no fixing money. I'll have nowt to pay you for my lodgings, Rachel."

"No," Mary Jane agreed, looking worried. "That's true enough."

Nelly went on eating steadily.

"Ey lass, haven't you enough to worry about?" Rachel shook her head. "Now drink up your tea honey, and stop getting yourself into such a bother over nowt. It's up to me to see that you get fixed up, if I'm worried about my rent money. But I'd cheerfully give food and a bed to Annie Lythe's lass without payment anytime. Now eat up and shut up, afore you get me cross."

I stared down at my plate then, feeling terrible. When I glanced back up at Mary Jane, my cheeks all hot and red, she grinned at me and winked. I picked up my bread and jam again.

"Thank you, Rachel," I said.

She touched my cheek and smiled.

We ate on in silence, till all at once a great commotion came from Trickey's cottage.

"Here they come," Rachel told us. "Wait for it! They've all been out parading round town in their best clothes today."

There was the tramp of feet on the stone cobbles outside, the sounds of loud voices and laughing; the floorboards started creaking and doors banged as the Scotch girls arrived back next door.

We smiled nervously at each other.

Mary Jane got up from the table and looked out of Rachel's kitchen window.

"Oh lor', Dory!" she squealed. "The boats ... the boats are setting off."

I jumped up, and ran to join her. "Our Robbie!" I said. "I meant to look for him and I'm too late."

"No you're not," Rachel told me. "Leave these pots, and run down the path to the ladder. You can get straight onto the pier from here, and watch the Whitby boats as they pass by. Go on! You'll have to hurry! You can wave to the *Whitby Rose* for me."

I ran down the path to the edge of the cliff, and I almost had to close my eyes as I walked across the narrow wooden bridge that Rachel called the ladder. It sloped down from the cliff edge to the pier, carrying us over a great space, with rocks beneath and the sea swilling back and forth as the tide turned. Mary Jane came pounding along behind me.

"Ooh ... I don't like crossing this," I called back to her.

"Just keep your Robbie in mind," she shouted.

I breathed out with relief as my feet touched the solid stone slabs of the pier and hurried on to the very end of it.

Two boats had passed already and most of the visiting fleet were already heading off to the fishing grounds.

"Oh let me see him … please let me see him," I whispered.

"Them's Penzancemen," Mary Jane shouted.

"How can you tell?" I screwed up my eyes to see better.

"You can tell by the double masts, and the PZ register mark on the side. Look!" she cried, hopping up and down beside me and pointing. "The *Whitby Rose*, David Welford's plosher. He's Rachel's husband … wave to 'im! Here's two Fifies with their brown sails and the sloping gaff rigg at the top. This un's from Lowestoft … see the cloth caps that the fellers wear."

"How do you know all that?" I asked, looking at Mary Jane with new respect.

"Our Sam's told me. He brought me last summer for the regatta. There he is… there he is now," she went frantic, waving and jumping up and down.

"Where? Where?" I begged, my head turning this way and that as the local boats passed quickly through the narrow harbour mouth and out into the open sea. They'd a steady westerly wind behind them.

"There," she yelled. "The *Esther Welford*."

"Oh yes," I waved along with her at the Welford brothers and Sam Ruswarp, but I was disappointed for I'd thought for a moment that she'd seen our Robbie.

Then, as the last few boats passed out between the arms of the two piers, I did see a young lad with a familiar look to him, in the stern of a sturdy Whitby plosher.

"Robbie!" I yelled at the top of my voice.

The lad turned towards us and it was our Robbie.

I ripped off my woollen shawl and waved it wildly over my head.

"Dory! Dory!" I heard him shout. He spoke to one of the men beside him and pointed to me and waved, but the boat was moving fast away. I waved and waved till it was out of sight.

146

147

"Did you see him?" I asked Mary Jane. "It was him, wasn't it?"

Mary Jane stared after the wake of the boats. "Oh aye, it was your Robbie, but did you see who he was with?" Her eyes were wide with surprise. "It was the *Louie Becket* he was on."

"The *Louie Becket*," I shook my head, it meant nowt to me. "I saw a big feller with a great bushy beard?"

"Aye. He's the old lifeboat man. You know the one … him as was the only one saved when the Whitby boat went down."

"Him?" I said. "Our Robbie's with the old lifeboat man?"

"Aye," she spoke quietly, impressed. "I think your Robbie's done all right for himself."

We ran back up to Henrietta Street, and told Rachel how we'd seen our Robbie. She laughed when she heard that

"I might of known," she said. "Wait till I tell Trickey! The old feller cannot resist the herring season. He's supposed to be retired and they've certainly retired him from his lifeboat work. He swore last summer that the herring catches were so poor, he'd not be going again."

"Well, there's no mistaking him," Mary Jane said. "And there was their Robbie as large as life on his boat."

"In that case, Dory, you can stop your fretting over Robbie," Rachel told me. "He couldn't be safer if he's on the *Louie Becket*, honey, and he'll be looked after, too. The old feller never had bairns of his own, and he's always had a fondness for the young 'uns."

"Yer'll not be sending him back to Sandwick now," said Nelly.

"No," I said. "I'll not even try."

I couldn't settle down to sleep that night, what with the strangeness of the room and Nelly snoring. The swish and lap of the sea was loud by our window, though the sound of it was a comfort to me.

We got up early next morning and bandaged up our fingers, for, as Rachel said, we had to look as though we meant business. Then we went straight round to the fish quay, carrying our oilies and boots.

Rachel spoke to two of the curer's men, but one said firmly that he'd more than enough. The other looked us up and down and said that I was nowt but a bairn.

"She's a big strong lass," said Rachel.

"Aye, she's tall, but I can see by her face she's a bairn. Look now," he said. "If I need another team I'll consider them, but I've all I need at the moment."

We hung around on the harbourside, watching the Scotch girls turning up for work in a noisy huddle as the boats began to arrive back, with a fair catch of gleaming herrings on board.

I looked out for Robbie, but I couldn't see him or the *Louie Becket*.

"Come on," said Rachel. "We'll go and get us a bite to eat, for there's nowt doing here."

We followed her back to Henrietta Street, feeling a bit down, and sat ourselves by the fire in Rachel's kitchen.

It was warm and spotlessly clean in there. Rachel had three freshly washed aprons drying by the fireside on a strange looking wooden clotheshorse with three spindly legs. I frowned at it; the washing reminded me of Mam, and there was something familiar about that clotheshorse.

We sipped the hot tea that Rachel handed out to us, and we were just beginning to unwind our bandaged fingers when there was a shout from the street and hammering on Rachel's door. Trickey came pounding up the hallway stairs.

"You want to get those lasses down to Pier Road," she shouted.

"What!" We all jumped up from our seats.

"There's a right old to-do," she panted, trying to get her breath, her eyes wide and excited.

"What's it all about?" Rachel asked.

"There's a Scotch lass sacked for bulking!"

"Now's your chance," Rachel cried, leaping up to grasp her shawl. "Get your oilies and boots and run as fast as you can wi' me."

We didn't need telling twice. We grabbed our things and pelted down through the streets to the bridge. But just as we got there, they closed the gates so that three tall-masted herring boats could pass through into the upper harbour.

We cursed and swore and jostled each other and jumped up and down on the spot.

"Look over there," Rachel cried, pointing to Pier Road. "I can tell there's trouble from here. Listen to them Scotch lasses shrieking?"

"What is it that they've done wrong?" I asked fearfully.

"Bulking," Rachel told me. "It's the packer that's at fault. She's been chucking the herrings into the barrels all anyhow, then covering it up with a neat layer at the top. They can fill the barrels quicker that way, but it's not allowed, the herrings don't keep so well. Oh no, you're sacked on the spot for bulking."

I caught my breath. It didn't seem such a terrible thing to me.

Then as soon as the bridge was open again, we were off running over it and down to Pier Road.

When we got close I slowed up, my heart pounding with fright. I didn't fancy taking the place of a girl who'd been sacked. All the gutters had stopped their work and they were bellowing and shouting and shaking their fists at the foreman. Their speech was so different that it was hard to understand, but their meaning was clear enough.

"Gi'er another chance, Willie!"

"Couldna ye give 'er another chance?"

"She's had all the chances she's going to get." The man wouldn't be budged.

"Then we sh'll come wi'ye, Maggie!" Another girl shouted.

"Aye. We'll nae work for ye Willie if Maggie's sacked. We'll be off to Scarborough. They're crying oot for lassies there. We wouldna stay wi'oot ye, Maggie!"

And suddenly there were three big lassies, unfastening their aprons and marching away from the long wooden farlanes of herrings.

Rachel was in there quick as a flash, pushing us forward. "You said my lasses could have the next chance."

"Aye," the foreman sighed and scratched his head. "So I did. I'll try them, but they'll be on their own. It's all Scotch lasses down here on Pier Road you know. The Whitby teams are by the upper harbour."

"We're not bothered," Nelly said.

"Well, they'll not be fixed till I see how they work. Right, lass," he pointed to me. "Get behind that farlane and let me see thee gip."

CHAPTER TEN

I struggled into my apron, my hands shaking horribly. I knew he'd picked on me because he thought I looked least able to do it. Quite a crowd had gathered about us.

"Look ye noo, he's teking on bairns," one of the Scotch girls muttered.

"Back to yer work," the man bellowed, and reluctantly the women turned again to their troughs.

I took the sharpest knife from my pocket and picked up a good-sized fish, trying hard to remember what Hannah had taught me. I pushed the knife in carefully and twisted it, and the guts flew out into the gut tub.

The man grunted. "Now size?" he snapped.

"Mattiefull," I answered him, my voice all shaky.

"What?" He put his hand to his ear.

"Mattiefull," I said it loudly.

He nodded and pointed to the basket behind me. I slipped the fish in and snatched up another herring to gut.

Nelly pushed in beside me and set to work. Mary Jane went to pack the barrel behind us.

"That one'll have to be packed again," the man said.

Mary Jane nodded, she began pulling the herrings out and setting them gently in a basket. One of the cooper lads went to help her.

I paused to watch Nelly for a moment and my mouth dropped open. Nelly could certainly gip, and she could gip fast. She'd done four fish while I did one.

"Stop gawping," she muttered under her breath. "Get gipping!"

"I'll try 'em for a week," the foreman told Rachel. "But that young un'll have to come into speed or she's out, and there'd better be no more bulking."

"Then I'll be needing a week's food and rent money," said Rachel, holding out her hand to him.

The herring catch wasn't huge, but by the time we'd emptied our farlanes at the end of the day, I felt as though I'd gipped the whole of the ocean.

My back ached, my legs ached, my hands were sore and swollen and I'd gathered three cuts that stung with the salt that the coopers sprinkled onto the herrings. Mary Jane and I took turns at packing and it brought us a bit of relief, though we had to pack the fish in perfect neat layers. The foreman kept watching us and checking in case we grew careless. All the while the Scotch girls frowned at us and looked on with suspicion.

One of the young coopers was kind to us. He was a strong, broad-built lad, who lifted the barrels as though they were bairns and whispered good advice that we gratefully took. The coopers' job was to make the barrels and see that they were carefully packed, with just the right amount of salt sprinkled between the layers of herrings. Then they'd stack the filled barrels up ready behind us for the herrings must be left to pickle for ten days.

I was so tired and hungry by midday that I thought I'd faint, and yet I knew that there was no stopping to eat or drink. I almost cried with relief at the sight of Rachel coming down Pier Road with a jug of warm broth and three bowls. It was the best broth I'd ever tasted, even though we had to take it in small quick sips while we stood at the farlanes.

Nelly gipped fast and steadily all through the day. She said little but she plodded on through the work like a donkey.

I was glad to have her there with us, and I knew how right Miriam had been when she called her a tough 'un.

"Is that it?" said Mary Jane, stretching and rubbing her back.

"Aye," said Nelly, carefully wiping her knives and putting them into her pocket.

"I thought I'd die," said Mary Jane. "I'm sore all over."

"My legs won't stop wobbling," I groaned. "I swear I can't walk back to Henrietta Street."

"Yer'll manage," said Nelly. "That were a slow day. I've seen 'em gip three times that lot."

"We'll want you back at six in t'morning, to help wi' topping up," the foreman told us. "Don't you be late!"

We rinsed our hands at the pump, and then set off walking slowly back to Rachel's house, a gang of the Scotch girls following behind us.

They shouted rude remarks at our backs and most of it I couldn't understand, but it was clear that they felt bitter about us taking the place of the girls that had gone, and I was scared of them.

At last, as we reached our door, one of the girls shouted out loudly so that we couldn't ignore it.

"You lot took Maggie's job fra her, we di'nna like that, ye ken. Bairns taking work fra those puir lasses that need the money."

I wanted to rush into Rachel's house and get away from them but Rachel herself opened the door. She'd clearly heard it all and she caught me by the arm.

"No, honey," she said. "We've to sort this out."

She marched up to the women, dragging me reluctantly along with her. Nelly and Mary Jane followed slowly.

"Now lasses," she said, "it's not as it seems. We didn't wish your Maggie sacked, but these lasses do need the money

154

bad. We had to grab at the chance. Dory's mam is sick, and cannot earn. Her father was drowned a few years back. Now you lasses know well what that means to a family."

The girls looked down and shuffled their feet.

Rachel went on, while I hung my head. "For this lass, it's the gipping or the workhouse. Aye and all her little brothers and sisters, too."

I took a deep breath and lifted my head to face them. "I didn't like to take your Maggie's job," I said loudly. "I didn't like it at all."

The Scotch girl sighed and nodded. "Di'nna fret, hinny. I do believe ye." She gently touched my cheek. "We'll forget it noo," she said.

"Aye, we'll forget it noo," the others agreed. They went quietly into Trickey's cottage.

"They'll be all right now," Rachel said, as we turned back to her door. "They're grand lassies really and wonderful the way they work. We don't like to fall out wi' them for they bring us good rent money each summer, and they don't ask much for it. Now," she said, back to her usual practical self, "oilies and boots outside and straight to your room. I'll fetch your water and your supper to you."

Nelly flopped down on her bed in all her muck, and lay like that until Rachel appeared with washing water and cloths and a good supper of fish stew.

"You surprised me, Dory!" Mary Jane grinned. "That were brave of you to speak up to them like that. It's not like you."

"Aye," I shook my head and smiled. "I don't know what come over me. My fingers hurt so much I didn't seem to care for owt else."

Nelly ate fast, then flopped back onto her bed again. Though I ached with each movement, I unwound the bandages and tried to wash my hands and put Mrs Love's ointment on my cuts.

"This water's going cold, Nelly, will you not wash?" I asked.

"No point," said Nelly and closed her eyes. "I'll wash meself on Sunday."

"Will you not change into your nightdress, Nelly?" Mary Jane asked, wrinkling her nose and pulling a face at me.

"Nobbut a waste o' time," Nelly muttered, already half asleep.

We were stiff as boards next morning when Rachel looked in to wake us.

"Come on," she called, grinning at the groans that came from us. "Aye, you'll be stiff I daresay, but there's only one way to be rid of it."

"What's that?" Mary Jane asked hopefully.

"Work on, hard and fast," Rachel told her.

That second day was even more difficult than the first, for the catch was good and we had to struggle through our stiffness and try to build up speed, but by the end of the day we all walked back to Henrietta Street feeling happier.

I was pleased for I'd seen our Robbie and he was mad with delight when he saw me gipping at the farlanes. He stood beside me for an hour or so chattering on and on about the fine time he was having fishing out of Whitby. I told him that I couldn't stop my work and he helped by pushing the herrings towards me.

"You should see them, Dory," he shouted. "You should see them silver darlings when we're scudding the nets. We haul them in, and they come flying at us, through the air and into the boat. They're everywhere! We're up to our knees in fish and covered in scales. And the smell, Dory! You wouldn't believe the smell!"

"Oh Robbie," I fussed. "Are you all right? Are you treated well?"

"Am I treated well?" he asked, a great smile on his face. "The old feller treats me like I'm his own lad. I make the tea for them," he said, beaming with importance. "And I make a good plum duff, boiled up in old condensed milk tins, for they need something warm and solid to fill their bellies out there."

"And can you do all that, Robbie?"

"Aye, I can. They've taught me how, and they never slap me if I spill. They just bellow at me and laugh."

"Oh Robbie," I worried. "It seems you've grown all of a sudden."

"Aye," he answered me sadly. "You've grown too, Dory. I would never have thought to see you working like this at the farlanes, and nagging at me just as if you were my mam."

Mary Jane was pleased that day too, for suddenly there was a face we all knew well, staring open-mouthed at us on the harbourside: Liza Welford, done up in smart nursemaid's clothes of good grey cloth all neatly buttoned. She'd a young boy dressed in a sailor suit held firmly by the hand on one side of her, and a tiny girl in silks and ribbons on the other side.

Mary Jane grinned and shouted. "I told you I could gip a herring, Liza Welford."

"I cannot believe my eyes," Liza gasped and stared at us, but the young boy pulled at her.

"Ice-cream," he shouted. "Want some ice-cream."

"Just a moment, Master Rupert," Liza spoke patiently. "These are my friends."

The boy looked up at us puzzled. "Are they tradespeople?" he demanded. "Phew! They smell! Mama says I mustn't speak to tradespeople. Stop talking to them and get me ice-cream. I'll tell Mama of you!"

Liza smiled rather sadly at us and shrugged her shoulders.

"I'll be back tomorrow," she called as the boy dragged her away.

We were glad to see her, and impressed by the elegance of her clothes, but we agreed that Liza did not seem at all happy. I'd never heard a young child speak to Liza like that. In our small school up at Bank Top, Liza Welford's word is law.

"What that one wants is a good hiding," Nelly said.

Nelly seemed to be in an unusually cheerful mood that day. She was quite chatty to us as we staggered our way back to Henrietta Street.

"Them Scotch lasses has been fine today," she said.

"Aye," I smiled. "That lass that shouted at us last night, she showed me how to drain off the pickle juice through the bunghole this morning, and she showed me how to pick the best fish for topping up the barrel. She was right kind to me and said to call her Jeanie."

"Aye," said Nelly, a secretive smile on her face. "And what about that big strong chap that works as our cooper. He says his name is George. He told me that as he filled our farlane and then he called me pet."

Mary Jane giggled. "He comes from Blythe. They call everyone pet up that way."

But the smile stayed there on Nelly's face.

"He called me pet," she said. "And he called me darling."

CHAPTER ELEVEN

We struggled on through the next few days, and by the time we'd cleared the farlanes on the Saturday night, we were dead on our feet.

"I'm gipped … as well as these herrings," Mary Jane grimaced at us, stretching to ease her back.

"I don't know what you're complaining about," said Nelly. "All these Scotch lasses are upset at the small catches."

Greater catches of herrings meant more money earned by us; for each team was paid by the number of barrels they managed to gut and pack. That week, I was grateful that the catches weren't huge for I couldn't have worked faster or harder than I did.

I grew to love the walk back to Rachel's cottage each night. Though my feet and my back ached and my fingers were swollen and stinging, still the relief at the end of the day was wonderful. Rachel's generous stews and puddings tasted as good as any fancy food we could dream up and the thought of them roused my spirits.

That first Saturday night, Jeanie's team, who'd been walking behind us, shouted wildly as we reached our door.

"What is it now?" I asked Mary Jane, nervously.

"I can't tell a word they're saying." She giggled as she wearily started to peel herself out of her smelly, crusted pinafore. "They get so excited and they talk so fast. If they'd only calm down and talk a bit slow."

It was Nelly that went to them. She listened frowning, then suddenly smiled back at us.

"Ceilidh?" she said. "Aye, I know what that means."

"What is it?" Mary Jane demanded.

"It's a bit of singing and dancing," Nelly told us, her eyes gleaming at the thought of it. "And the coopers are coming over to Tate Hill Pier."

We rushed then to get out of our oilies, and kicked off our boots by Rachel's doorstep.

After we'd had our supper we made good use of the washing water that Rachel brought to us, and got ourselves as clean and tidy as we could. Then we hurried down to Tate Hill Pier.

At first we sat and listened to a band playing on the far side of the harbour. The strains of music and the steady beat of the drum came to us clearly across the calm water.

We could see the coopers gathered by the bandstand and some of the Scotch girls. They'd lodgings on the Crag, on the Westside, where they rented little rooms like ours from the fishermen's wives. Most of them were packed five or six into a room, and I knew that our lodgings with Rachel were spacious beside theirs. They kept waving at us, and when the bandsmen packed away their instruments and left, the coopers and the lasses came over the bridge to join us. Two of the lads had brought their squeeze boxes and another had a mouth organ. They settled themselves on the solid stone slabs of Tate Hill Pier and began playing tunes that were familiar to us all. It wasn't long before the fishermen came leaping ashore from their boats to join in with the singing.

There were Cornishmen, Scotchmen, and the Lowestoft men in their best Norfolk jackets and cloth caps. There were others like our cooper George who'd come down from Northumberland. They chattered and sang together in their different voices, making a fine and funny mixture of sounds.

Nelly was full of cheek and asked George outright if he were married.

He shook his head and smiled.

"Are yer courtin' then?" she demanded.

"Why no, pet," he said. "Are y' offering?"

Nelly suddenly went quiet and pink in the cheeks, while all the fellows laughed and hooted. I'd never seen Nelly look shamed before.

It was a beautiful summer evening; still and warm. I forgot my tiredness and wished that it would go on forever. Even the old women came out from their cottages and sat by the harbourside knitting and nodding their heads to the tunes they played. As dusk fell, lamps were lit everywhere, for all the boats had crowded into the harbour for the weekend. The golden shimmer of their riding lights reflected in the water and the boats creaked gently as they rocked up and down to the wash of the waves.

Our Robbie came running down over Tate Hill sands with the old lifeboatman striding after him.

"I've found our Dory!" he yelled, and flung his arms round me. The old fellow went to gossip with Trickey and Rachel who'd brought their knitting outside.

The singing and clapping grew loud and jolly and some of the lasses got up and danced.

George held out his hand to Nelly. "Come Nelly, dance wi' me, pet. I never meant to give offence."

Nelly didn't need asking twice.

Soon me and Mary Jane were skipping along with them, though I don't know where the energy came from. One young Scotch girl sat alone and would not join in.

"What's up wi' her," I nudged Mary Jane and pointed.

"She's one o' them that's come down from Stornaway," said Mary Jane. "See her black scarf. Jeanie told me she only speaks the gaelic."

I stared at her. I could see from her face that she was young, no older than me. I was homesick enough, just coming down from Sandwick. I couldn't imagine what it must be like to travel so far from your home to such mucky work.

"Jeanie, Jeanie," I called as she whirled past with one of the coopers. "Will the Stornaway lass not dance?"

"Och, Katrina," Jeanie shook her head. "The poor bairn's nae left her home afore. We try oor best to look after her, but her faither has made her promise to keep herself away fra the laddies. She keeps to her word like a wee saint."

"Poor soul!" said Mary Jane. "Will she dance with us? We're not the laddies?"

"Ye canna do harm to try," Jeanie nodded.

So we went and stood in front of Katrina and we held out our hands to her. At first she would not budge, but as we kept on at her, with daft bits of miming and prancing around, at last she giggled and gave in. We took both of her hands and skipped round together until she was pink-cheeked and laughing.

"How can I skip like this when my feet hurt so?" I yelled at Mary Jane.

"I can't feel my feet at all," she grinned.

When at last we could stand no more, we flopped down by Robbie who sat with the lifeboatman.

"I wish Liza Welford were here to see all this," said Mary Jane. "Would they let her out on a Saturday night, do you think?"

I shook my head. I somehow didn't think that they would.

"I wonder if she can hear all this singing, up in her fine room," I said.

Just at that moment we seemed to have more in common with a Stornaway fisherlass who couldn't even speak to us, than any of those fine English folk who stayed up there on the West Cliff. The dancing faded out, and Jeanie stood up to sing.

"Who'll buy my fresh herrin' they're bonny fish and wholesome farin'.
Who'll buy my fresh herrin' new pulled from the sea.
When you were sleeping on your pillows, did you think of our poor fellows?
Darkling with the wildest billows, pulling herrin' from the sea.
Who'll buy my fresh herrin' ..."

She'd a lovely deep voice and we all listened quietly, and clapped her when she stopped.

"We sing out there, you know," said Robbie, his eyes bright in the oil lamp's glow.

"What, you sing at sea?"

"Oh aye," he said, "but singing is quite different out there, Dory. It makes me want to cry."

"Nay, Robbie. Why should it make you cry?"

"It's the quiet of the sea all around us. First we have the fuss of shooting the nets, but then we have to settle down and wait. It goes very quiet, Dory ... too quiet, and that's when they start. One of the Cornishmen will pick out the tune on his accordion, and we listen for a bit, then one of the chaps will start to sing, and we listen again, then slowly, slowly we join in. The sound o' deep voices comes from all the distant boats and it grows and grows until the whole fleet is singing."

"Oh Robbie," I cried. "It sounds beautiful."

"Aye, it's grand," he said, shaking his head. "But they only sing hymns out there. I don't think it would seem right to sing owt else."

"Oh, I wish I could hear it," I said.

The old lifeboatman who'd been listening to us, leaned forwards and touched my arm. "Don't you fret, little lass.

You shall hear the Cornishmen singing their hymns, for I believe they've arranged to have a service on the boats tomorrow."

Sunday was a quiet day, and even Nelly kept to her word and had a good wash, though we knew the smell of herrings still clung to us and would not be washed away, however many rinses of fresh water Rachel brought. We dressed ourselves in our Sunday clothes and gathered by the harbour-side to listen to the lovely sounds of the Cornishmen singing their hymns, just as the old fellow had promised. They'd carried a harmonium out onto Tate Hill Pier, and Mary Jane edged closer and closer to it. I saw her fingers twitching to the solemn rhythm of the hymns, her face lit up with pleasure.

When they'd finished, we went to help Rachel with the dinner. I'd never had such a fine meal in all my life. Rachel and her husband had invited John Jack Trevorrow, the skipper of one of the Cornish luggers who'd been coming to Whitby for many years, and us three lasses sat at the table with them in our Sunday-best clothes.

Like all the fishermen's wives, Rachel had her ornaments and brasses polished and displayed for Sunday. Her kitchen looked a treat, with the black-leaded cooking range shining like jet, and the strange wooden drying rack folded away neatly in the fire corner.

As soon as we'd finished our dinner, Rachel sent us down to John Jack's boat, the Silver Star, to carry roast beef and a jug of gravy to the four men and the young cook who made up his crew.

Mary Jane pulled faces at me.

"We're never going to get Nelly away from these Cornish lads," she mouthed.

But she was wrong, for though the Cornish lads were full

of fun and cheek, Nelly was not her usual loud-mouthed, forward self.

Later that afternoon, we set off with Jeanie's gang, marching arm-in-arm up the Abbey stairs to look down on the town from the top of the East Cliff. When we'd had our fill of the fine view from up there, we set off to parade ourselves round town; then last of all we climbed the steep hill up onto the West Cliff. All the other gipping girls did the same, and we yelled and cheered at the tops of our voices when we saw another gang of herring gutters coming towards us.

We caught a glimpse of Liza up near the Saloon Gardens with her charges. We greeted her loudly, but she seemed flustered.

"I've been told I've not to speak to you, nor any trades people," she whispered, her cheeks red with the shame of it.

This was not the brave Liza Welford that we all knew. I hated to see her so timid and anxious.

The boy pulled at her arm and pinched his nose rudely. "Mama said no speaking to stinky fish girls," he cried. "Get me more lemonade or I'll tell Mama."

Liza ignored him for a moment. "I've to take them both to the picture man's studio tomorrow," she said. "They're to have their portraits made."

"It's a good job he's a patient man," said Mary Jane. "Even he might have a job to make that one look sweet."

"Best go now," said Liza.

"Did you see that?" Mary Jane spoke furiously as Liza went off towards the gardens.

"What?" I stared about us.

"He kicked her. That spoilt brat of a child kicked our Liza on purpose, and she did nothing."

"I told you," said Nelly. "He needs a good clout."

"I'd throw the lemonade right in his face!" cried Mary Jane.

We went to chapel with Rachel for the evening service, and found it filled with Cornishmen. Their voices swelled the singing and made it very fine. We didn't argue with Rachel when she insisted that we should get an early night, even though we knew that Monday should be a quiet day for the men would never go out fishing on a Sunday night

CHAPTER TWELVE

On Monday we slept till seven o'clock, then went to help the coopers sort out the barrels ready to go to the railway station, for there was still work to do. We had to open up the bung holes to drain off the salty oil and fish juices from the barrels that had stood there pining and pickling for more than a week. Then we had to top the barrels up with more herrings and pour back the pining juice till they were full and tightly packed, with a layer of perfect herrings on the top and straw to protect them.

"Ye canna get a finer handcream than the pining juice," Jeanie told us.

She made us dabble our hands in the smelly stuff and rub it well in. Though it made my cuts sting for a while, I found she was right, for as it seeped in, my skin grew soft and supple.

George pegged down the barrel lids carefully. He patted the top fondly, proud of a well-made barrel, filled and finished just right.

"They'll keep for a good twelve month now," he said. "It's off you go for a nice train ride, my fine fat silver darlings."

We giggled for he sounded as though he spoke to his bairns, or even his sweetheart.

"Hey Nelly! You'd better watch out," said Mary Jane, full of sauciness. "This lad's in love with the little fishes."

Monday was an easier day, with no herrings arriving. There was no need to bandage up our fingers and our work was done by noon. So we went back to Henrietta Street and helped Rachel to cover all her ornaments for the week's work.

"I hear you want to knit a gansey, honey," Rachel said. "A gansey for your brother. I'd say he deserves it too."

"I would…" I answered wistfully.

She kindly gave me knitting needles and a few skeins of wool to start me off and we settled then to do our knitting by the harbourside, gossiping and watching the men load up the boats with food, and freshly mended nets.

The weeks fell into a hard pattern of work, though Sunday and Monday brought us some relief. I managed to come into a bit of speed, and the foreman agreed to keep us on till the season in Whitby ended. Though I managed to gip the herrings faster, I could not come anywhere near to the Scotch girls.

"Well noo," boasted Jeanie. "When ye've worked at the gipping as long as me, ye'll tern oot fifty or sixty herrin' a minute."

"Aye, so you say, so you say," said Nelly gutting steadily.

But we knew that Jeanie was not far wrong.

Dan Welford came to the farlanes looking for us. He was pleased to see that we'd got work, and he told me that all was well at home and that my mam was certainly no worse.

Sometimes we'd have an early morning visit from the picture man. He'd turn up with his new box cameras slung about his neck, and he'd be there beside the farlanes just as we were getting going, or late in the evening when we were packing up. He took snap-shot pictures of us, as he called them, while we chatted to him, though we dare not stop our work to help him with his pictures.

"You should come to take our pictures at noon when the sun's bright and we're piled high with herring," we told him.

He smiled and shook his head. "I've an appointment to

make a picture of a bouncing baby at noon," he said sadly, and looked at his watch and left.

The first time that he saw us, he bowed in surprise and raised his hat.

"Herring ladies from Sandwick, I believe."

Mary Jane giggled and smiled broadly. "Do you remember, sir, how you took my picture once, sitting on Plosher Rock along with Liza Welford? The print you gave us has pride of place on Mam's mantelpiece."

"How could I ever forget?" he said. "That picture won me a medal. It was the beauty of the models that did it, of course."

That made Mary Jane giggle even more.

The first few weeks of August seemed to pass very fast, though sometimes I'd get a tightness in my stomach, that brought a terrible homesickness with it. It came when I thought about my mam and Alice and the bairns, but the work was so hard that there just wasn't time to sit and fret about it, and at least I saw that our Robbie was safe and well.

It was the last week in August when the change came. The catches were down and there were a lot of anxious folk about. We all stood to lose from poor catches; the dealers, the curers, the fishermen, the coopers and the gipping girls. Then we had four terrible days, one after another, when the catch was downright poor.

Everyone was thrown into despair. The dealers were talking of giving up and moving down to Grimsby. The fishermen's wives were most upset at that; if the fleet moved south so early, the herring girls and coopers would have to follow them and they'd lose the rent money that they got as landladies. I was fearful, for I knew I'd be shamed to go back to Sandwick Bay with such a small amount of money to show for my efforts.

"Aye. It's not like it used to be, honey," Rachel told me. "It's all fading away. There were summers when I were a lass that the herrings were so plentiful we didn't need the bridge to get us across Whitby Harbour."

I must have looked puzzled for Rachel laughed. "We didn't need the bridge see, for there were so many boats all crowded into the harbour that you could cross the water just by stepping from boat to boat"

"No!" said Mary Jane. "Can that be really true?"

"I swear it's no lie," Rachel told us. "Folk just walked from one boat to another, especially at weekends. And there were days when the barrels of herrings were piled so high in Whitby streets that they had to put on special trains to carry them away. There were hundreds of wagonloads leaving for market every week."

"Then why are the catches so poor now?" I asked.

"My husband swears that it's these big new steam trawlers, dredging up the herring young and making it hard for the smaller boats."

Suddenly we found that we were spending our days by the harbourside, watching the comings and goings, and the gansey that I was knitting our Robbie grew fast from my needles.

Fishermen stood around the harbour rail fretting and discussing the weather and the wind and the swimming of the shoals. The weather was hot, too hot some said. Too calm and still and heavy.

The Whitby men and those from Lowestoft were talking about fishing on Sunday to see if they could make up their losses. The Cornishmen were shocked at that and the Scotchmen didn't like it at all.

At last it was decided that the Cornishmen should hold a special prayer meeting in the Old Primitive Methodist

Chapel, and it was agreed that there'd be no more talk of Sunday fishing till after the service.

We were sitting on Tate Hill Pier that evening, doing our knitting and wondering whether we should attend the service or whether it were best left to the Cornishmen, when the picture man came wandering up the beach, carrying his heavy black camera box. He walked slowly and he seemed to be looking behind the rocks and peeping into the boat sheds.

"Have yer lost summat?" Nelly shouted to him.

He looked up at us and smiled, scratching his head.

"I know it's ridiculous," he said. "But I've lost my legs."

We all giggled for he looked to have a fine pair of legs to us.

He laughed with us. "Wooden legs, camera legs." He chuckled. "I swear that I left a set of camera legs somewhere near Tate Hill Pier. It was a dreadful day, poured with rain, and I stashed them somewhere meaning to come back for them."

All of a sudden it came to me in a flash that I knew exactly where the camera legs were hidden. Rachel's clotheshorse that aired her washing by the fire had always looked somehow familiar to me. Now I knew why, they were just like the folding wooden camera legs that I'd carried for the picture man, that day when we watched the herring fleet arrive, from the bank top at Sandwick Bay.

My mouth dropped open and my hand flew up to cover it

"What's wrong?" Mary Jane asked. "You look as if you've seen a ghost!"

"I know," I said all blushing and excited. "I know where your camera legs are, sir, but I don't know what Rachel will say."

I explained it to him and he looked amused.

ACKNOWLEDGEMENTS

I have tried to make the details of the fisherwomen's lives as realistic as possible and in my efforts to do this I have found the following books and articles very helpful and informative:

Frank Meadow Sutcliffe, Photographer: A Selection of His Work compiled by Bill Eglon Shaw, published by the Sutcliffe Gallery

Frank Meadow Sutcliffe: A Second Selection compiled by Bill Eglon Shaw, published by the Sutcliffe Gallery

Frank Meadow Sutcliffe: A third selection compiled by Michael Shaw, published by the Sutcliffe Gallery

The Nagars of Runswick Bay by J.S. Johnson, published by Runswick Bay Publications

Mary Linskill: 1840–1891 by Cordelia Stamp, published by Caedmon of Whitby

Mary Linskill: The Whitby Novelist by David Quinlan and Arthur F. Humble, published by Home and Son Ltd

Yorkshire Fisherwomen, an article based on the work of Peter Frank, published by the Spare Rib Co-operative

*YORKSHIRE FISHERFOLK by Peter Frank, was published by PHILLIMORE & Co. LTD in 2002. This social history of

the Yorkshire inshore fishing community was published after *THE FLITHER PICKERS* and *THE HERRING GIRLS* first appeared. It is a clear, detailed and well-illustrated account and it is highly recommended by the author to readers who would like to know more on the subject.

The Green Howards by Geoffrey Powell, published by Hamish Hamilton

Following the Fishing by David Butcher, 1987 (Tops'l Books)

Close to the Earth by Judith Cook, (Routledge & Kegan Paul)

Fishing out of Whitby by John Tindale, 1987 (Dalesman)

The author would also like to acknowledge the kind help and advice given to her by Mr John Tindale, Mrs Anne Leadley and Mr Bill Fortune, Also information and advice from Whitby Library and Whitby Literary and Philosophical Society.

The final photograph of Herring Girls is by an unknown photographer – and published with permission from North Yorkshire Archives.

The photograph of the Washerwoman is by Sutcliffe and published with permission from Bradford Museum of Film and Photography.

"A drying rack, you say?"

We all got up then, smiling about it, and we led the picture man back to Henrietta Street. Rachel herself was there, just finishing the whitening of her doorstep.

"There y'are" she said, and she bobbed to the picture man. "I've a kettle just boiling," she told him. "Won't you come in and take a cup of tea, sir. I were just about to make some for the lasses."

"That's most kind of you," he said, and we all trooped into Rachel's kitchen, and sat ourselves down. There, in front of the fire, was the strange drying rack with a couple of Rachel's petticoats slung over it to air.

The picture man clearly recognised his camera legs, and he nodded at me and smiled while Rachel made the tea. Then we all sat there, chatting on about the lack of herrings, while we sipped at our tea and waited for the picture man to mention the drying rack.

At last he got up to go and he'd still said nothing to Rachel about it. I was puzzled as to what to do when Mary Jane came to the rescue.

"Rachel," she said. "He don't like to tell you, but the gentleman has lost his camera legs, and there they are in front of the fire, airing your petticoats."

"What!" Rachel went quite red and flustered.

"Pray don't upset yourself, dear lady," the picture man said. "I find I don't need them after all, and you have discovered such a good use for them. I'd be pleased if you'd keep them."

"Oh heavens!" said Rachel, crossing the room and whisking her petticoats off the wooden camera legs. "Why ever did I not realise? I found them down by Dryden's boatshed. I thought the tide had washed them up. I was sure I'd find a use for them for they're made of good strong varnished wood."

"And you have found a use for them. As good a use as I. I'd be delighted if you'd keep them now."

Rachel hesitated just for a moment, but then she firmly folded up the camera legs and handed them to the picture man, smiling comfortably now.

"You take them back," she said. "For I can air my petticoats on any old piece of wood, but you need these to fix up that camera of yours."

He took them then, and thanked her for the tea, and went off happily down Henrietta Street. We laughed when he'd gone.

"I thought he were never going to take them," said Mary Jane.

"Ey dear," said Nelly. 'He's a daft 'un. Fancy not wishing to tek his own belongings."

"Not daft," said Rachel. "Not daft at all. He's what I call a proper gentleman."

CHAPTER THIRTEEN

We went along with Rachel and her husband to the prayer meeting, but we could not even get inside, the chapel was so crowded. We stood out on the street and joined in the singing. The Cornishmen were in good voice and we sang for all we were worth.

My eyes filled up with tears as the service finished with the hymn my dad loved best of all. I remembered how he used to bellow out the words in his deep voice at the back of our small chapel in Sandwick Bay, so that folk turned round to look at him, and Mam would stick her elbow in his side to quiet him down a bit.

The powerful words and music poured out of the small chapel and filled the streets and alleyways.

Will your anchor hold in the straits of fear,
When the breakers roar and the reef is near;
While the surges rave, and the wild winds blow,
Shall the angry waves then your bark o'er flow?
We have an anchor that keeps the soul,
Steadfast and sure while the billows roll;
Fastened to the rock which cannot move,
Grounded firm and deep in the saviour's love!

As we walked back to Henrietta Street, it turned cooler and a chilly wind started to blow.

"Well, my honey, let us hope all that singing and praising does some good," Rachel said, and I silently echoed her prayer.

David Welford sniffed at the wind. "This breeze comes off the heather," he said. "A good north-westerly, I swear.

Maybe these Cornishmen know what they're about."

"Well," said Mary Jane. "I've never known prayers answered fast as that."

The wind grew strong, and the town was filled with excitement. Some of the herring boats put out to sea at once, though others hesitated, fearing it might turn into a gale.

As the blast grew stronger and the sea rough, the herring drifters that were anchored out in the sea roads ran for the safety of the harbour. The tide was on the turn and it would not be long before the shallow water would make the harbour entry difficult. We wrapped our shawls around us tight, and stood up on the cliffside watching them.

"By the heck!" David Welford said. "When these Cornishmen sing up a storm, they don't muck about"

As dusk fell, two luggers and three of the bigger coble boats that had bravely gone out to sea as soon as the wind rose were seen heading back through rough water.

We ran along to the cliff ladder to see them better.

Mary Jane clutched my arm. "Dear God!" she cried. "Look at that!"

The sea swilled through the space beneath the cliff ladder with a violent force even though the tide was going out. The luggers made the harbour safely, and the three cobles following came steadily towards the welcoming outstretched arms of the harbour. The small boats were tossed fiercely as the waves grew, it was hard going for them, we could all see that, and I clenched my fists up tight as we watched them.

"Can we not do summat?" I said.

Suddenly a rocket was fired on the far side of the harbour.

"See!" cried Rachel, pointing to the beach beyond the West Pier. "Thomas Langlands has called the lads to launch the lifeboat."

"Aye," her husband had to shout, for the wind snatched his voice away. "They've got a job on mind. I wonder whether to go to help. They'll be done by the time I get round there."

"You stay put," Rachel told him firmly. "They've plenty o' lads, and look – they're already off."

We watched from our vantage point where the ladder joined the cliff as they hauled the lifeboat on its carriage towards the slipway. We lost sight of them then, but we knew that the launchers would soon be up to their waists in swirling water.

"Ah," David sighed, as we caught a glimpse of the boat as it breasted the waves. "They're off! He's done well, has Thomas."

I was frightened standing out there, so near the cliff edge. The force of the wind drummed away behind us, pushing us closer to that edge at every blast, but I couldn't go back till we'd seen the cobles safely in.

The lifeboat stood by, and a cheer went up from the great crowd of watchers that had gathered as the first coble reached the safety of the harbour mouth. But almost at once a dreadful groan came from all around, for the two following cobles had been knocked sharply off-course as two cutting waves collided and rose high into the air. For a sickening moment both the boats were lost to our sight.

I cried out loud and grabbed tight hold of Mary Jane's shoulder. "Are they over?"

"Nay," she said. "But they're like to be."

Then we saw them again, both boats had missed the harbour mouth and been driven behind the great bulk of the East Pier close below us.

"The rocks!" David Welford cried. "They'll run aground. They cannot get the lifeboat round there, too shallow by far. We'll have to drag 'em off, Rachel."

And with that he was leaping down the precarious cliff ladder, over the water that crashed through the gap and down to the pier.

"Fetch them lassies from Trickey's house!" Rachel shouted to us. Then she hurried after her husband.

"I'll get them," Nelly cried.

"Come wi' me," Mary Jane bellowed and she snatched at my arm. "They'll be needing a great gang for this." Then she started to run down the cliff ladder after Rachel.

I heard cries, shouts, and the sound of running feet behind me. People were pounding their way up Henrietta Street and heading for the ladder; they'd all be needed if there were to be any hope of dragging the boats away from the rocks and keeping the coblemen out of the wretched sea.

I stepped onto the wooden ladder and made myself move forward, though it rocked with the fierce wind. Then I froze as I looked down at the drop beneath me, as the sea roared and slavered below me like an angry starving beast.

I knew I must move on, for folk were coming up fast behind me and I thought I might be thrown over the side in the panic and rush, but the drop was so deep and the sea so wild that terror gripped me. It was Rachel that made me move. I think she'd seen that I was stuck, all iced-up with fear.

"Dory!" she cried. "Get down here now! It's the *Louie Becket*! We need you here!"

That was it! That did it! Our Robbie was on that boat. I couldn't leave Robbie to be tossed into the sea, or crushed on those rocks. I stepped forward and, though the ladder seemed to swing wildly, I stared ahead through the gloom and the gale, making myself walk on till at last I stepped out onto the solid slabs of the pier.

David Welford had managed to snatch up a rope that they'd thrown from the *Louie Becket*. He handed it to Rachel, and then went teetering on the edge of the pier to catch a rope from the second boat.

"Help me!" Rachel shouted, lurching towards the pier side, dragged by the weight of the boat and the strength of the waves.

We ran! Mary Jane grabbed at the rope and I clung onto Rachel, gripping her round the waist. I caught a glimpse of our Robbie's white face below us. He was clinging to the side of the boat.

"Never fear," Rachel bellowed in my ear. "I can see 'em both. The old feller has hold of your brother by the braces."

All I could do was cry out stupidly. "It's me as stitched those braces."

"Let's pray you stitched 'em well," cried Mary Jane.

We struggled to hang on tight for what seemed like ages, but at last when Trickey arrived with Jeanie and the Scotch girls, we knew that we'd enough help to keep the rope safe, and we started to haul the coble towards the tip of the pier.

As we rounded the tip we had to be careful and listen well to David, who told us when to pull and when to stop, for we'd so many folk on the pier all heaving and hauling that we were in danger of falling into the sea ourselves. The old lifeboatman and his men kept the *Louie Becket* clear of the stone built pier with their oars. Robbie was grinning and yelling with excitement, while the plosher pitched and tossed in the darkening water. I don't think he knew what danger he was in.

When at last we had the Louie Becket safe inside the harbour, I ran straight up the cliff ladder without a thought, and down to the sands where people had gathered to help the men out. I ran to them, careless as to whether the second coble was saved or not.

Once we'd got them safely up to Henrietta Street, the women flung open their warm kitchens to the drenched fishermen. Robbie and the old feller were soon sitting by Rachel's fireside, wrapped in warm dry blankets sipping broth.

I hugged my brother, while he grinned at me.

"Oh Robbie, I was so scared for you."

"Aye," said Mary Jane. "All she'd do was fret about your braces."

"Now Robbie," the old fellow chuckled, and wiped the broth from his beard. "I've always said braces is unlucky on a fisherman, but it seems that yours have saved your life."

Though the storm carried on and the noise of the wind wouldn't let us sleep, Rachel sent us off to our beds, saying that Robbie and the old feller must stay till morning. We lay there whispering restlessly until a great crash and the sound of splintering wood sent us jumping out of our beds in the early hours. We ran to the small window near my bed and stared out through the dim light of dawn. The wind had dropped, but we could see the great mast of a ship, tilted to the side, down beside the pier. Again a loud cracking sound was heard and the mast juddered. It was clear that another ship had run aground.

"Rachel, Rachel," we called. "We must go down again. There's men will need help."

"Nay," Rachel shouted to us, coming into our room fully dressed with a bucket in each hand. She laughed and shook her head. "They don't need saving. Thomas Langlands and his crew have got them off and they're safe ashore. It's the ship breaking up that's banging and cracking so, and she's a collier. The tide is going out. Now you know what that means, don't you, lasses?"

We all three smiled broadly. "Free coal!"

"Right," said Rachel. "Are you fit to help us then, for they'll all be down there … fast as you can say knife?"

We flung on our clothes and Rachel handed out buckets and baskets and sacks, but though we'd not wasted any time, we found that half of Whitby was down there by the rocks, slipping and sliding and grubbing about, up to their thighs in blackened water.

All through the morning we clambered over the rocks picking up lumps of wet coal. By noon there was not a scrap of it left, though there were damp black trails all through the streets and alleyways, and folk with smeared faces, and hands and arms and aprons. Bairns carried baskets of coal to their grannies and everywhere there were smiling faces.

"They say God works in a mysterious way," said Rachel, with a laugh. "We ask for fish and he gives us coal. Now we've hope of keeping warm right through next winter."

The shiny black stuff was as good as lumps of gold, and whether the Cornishmen had sung up a storm of fishes or not, everyone was glad.

When the fleet set off that evening, there was a good crowd down on the piers to watch them go, with a steady westerly wind behind them. I stood there waving to our Robbie as he passed in the *Louie Becket*.

"Oh, I wish he wasn't going," I said. "Not after last night."

Mary Jane shrugged her shoulders. "It's their last chance," she said. "The dealers will surely move on, if there's no better catch in the morning."

We slept well that night, for the wind had dropped and we were exhausted with all the upset and excitement that we'd had. Next morning we were up early and waiting hopefully at the farlanes before ever there was any sign of the boats coming in.

The dealers were restlessly walking up and down Pier Road, and the coopers and gippers all there and ready to work. At last there were shouts from the pier, and the sound of cheering. Most of the folk went running off down towards the harbour mouth.

"We should stay by the farlanes and wait," said Nelly.

"I'm not," said Mary Jane.

"I can't wait," I said, and hurtled off after her down towards the pier, pushing my way through the crowd.

There was a fine sight, all the drifters heading steadily back to harbour, mobbed by gangs of hungry herring gulls that wheeled and screeched above them. One of the Whitby ploshers led them all.

"Look," Mary Jane yelled. "Look it's the *Louie Becket*."

I screamed out loud, bursting with pride, for there was our Robbie standing in the bows, up to his knees in a huge pile of gleaming herrings.

"Robbie! Robbie," we yelled, jumping up and down.

"Silver darlings!" he shouted. "Hundreds of 'em, thousands of 'em."

CHAPTER FOURTEEN

We had to run back fast to our farlanes then, for we'd be sacked if we were not there when the coopers came to fill them up.

It was a wild day that followed, what with dealers competing for the fish and the prices going up and up and us gipping away forever. The farlanes were piled high like I'd never seen them, and the smart visitors came down the steep pathways to gawp at us. They milled around, asking daft questions and getting in our way.

Though we were already tired by noon, there was such a spirit of rejoicing that I could not feel miserable. It was a warm sunny day and as we worked the fish seemed to fly through our hands. Glints of deep purple and blue glanced up into our eyes from the pattern of black diamonds on the herrings' backs, while the bright midday sun caught their creamy white underbellies, making them gleam with rainbow lights like mother of pearl.

"Treasure…" I murmured.

"Treasure all right," Nelly agreed with me for once. "Good as silver coins these are."

I went into a waking dream, my hands working of their own accord, not noticing any more the strong oily smell of fish and the dark red blood of the guts that spattered my face and arms.

When dusk fell we'd still got our farlanes piled high, and the fleet had set out to try their luck once more. George and the other coopers set up oil lamps between the farlanes so that we could see as it grew dark.

It started to rain and though we got soaked to our skins, still we gipped the herrings.

"How long must we go on?" I begged Jeanie.

"We've tae work till we've done, lassie," she told me.

It was then that exhaustion really hit me, I felt as though someone had been beating me over the shoulders, leaving me bruised and sore. I looked down and saw properly just what I stood amongst. My father's best sea boots were deep in fish guts so that I could not see them clear, my apron the same, and my arms crusted up to the elbows. Nelly stood beside me, crusted and filthy, steadily gipping away.

"Oh Jeanie," I said. "I cannot do it. I cannot gip another fish."

"Ye canna stop noo, lassie," she told me cheerfully. "Keep going, and we'll have a bit of a sing, tae cheer us. Turn the lamps up, George!"

The warm golden glow lifted my spirits, though the sooty smuts from the smoking lamps blew into our faces. Jeanie got us singing fast and loud.

"Halibut for the swanky squire,
Haddock for his wife,
Cod is for the parson,
Mackerel for long life.
Ling is for the fisherman,
Fish head stew for free,
But the bonny salted herring,
Is the only fish for me!"

We all joined in, smiling and laughing. The rhythm and the tune seemed to help us and, as our voices grew loud and rough, we gipped faster than ever.

"Oh, we are jolly herring girls,
A-salting all day through.
We salt the silver darlings,

And we'll do the same to you.
Oh, we are jolly herring girls,
A-gipping all day through,
We gip the silver darlings,
And we'll do the same to you.
Oh, we are jolly herring girls,
A-pickling all day through.
We pickle the silver darlings,
And we'll do the same to you."

The song finished with wild cheers and screaming. At last, with thick darkness gathering around the glow of our oil lamps, we could see that we were coming to the end and emptying our farlanes.

I can't remember the walk back to Henrietta Street, though I seem to think that Rachel was with us. I think she must have carried us back. What I do know is that we all slept in our filthy clothes that night, glad of the bare rooms and brown paper covered curtains. None of us washed till the morning, and we didn't bother over-much then.

Next day the catches were up again, though not quite as much of a miracle as the day before. Though we ached and grumbled, everyone told us that the only way to get right was to work on, and so we did. It was at noon that day that we had a terrible bit of excitement.

The usual gang of visitors was gathering about to watch us at work, and even the picture man had deserted his studio to struggle through the crowd to make his snap-shots. Then we saw Liza Welford, there with her two charges.

"Liza! Liza!" Mary Jane shouted happily, though she never stopped her packing. "I thought the smelly fisherlasses were forbidden."

"Aye. So they are, but I don't care, I'm not missing this."

That sounded much more like the Liza that we all knew. She stood at the back of the crowd, holding the little lass up to watch our work. The boy climbed up beside her, close to the harbour rail pulling at her and whining as usual, though I could see that Liza told him to get down.

I was glad that I paused just for a moment in my work to smile across at them, for it was then it happened and I saw it clearly. One minute the lad was there, scratching and hot in his expensive sailor suit, the next he wasn't, and all I could see was the space by the harbour rail where he'd been.

I dropped the herring that I was gutting and I screamed at the top of my voice.

"Liza! The lad! He's fallen in the water!"

George had been sprinkling our fish with salt. He looked up at me as I screamed and just for one moment he stared into my face with horror, then he turned about and I've never seen anyone move so fast. He cut straight through the pushing crowd, leaping up onto the harbour rail, and vanished from sight after the boy.

"George!" A great frightened bellow went up beside me from Nelly. Then everyone rushed to the harbour rail.

The tide was in and the water was cold and deep, but George had the lad by the collar of his suit. The child came up, choking and spouting dirty harbour water, but George swam quickly to the nearest steps and they were both hauled out of the water by many willing hands. It was all over in a minute, and the big man was standing dripping on the quayside with the spluttering shivering lad in his arms.

"Liza! Where's Liza?" Mary Jane turned about, looking for her friend.

Though everyone else had stopped their work and rushed to the harbour side, Liza had not moved. She stood just where she'd been before, her face gone white as a ghost. She clutched the little lass so tightly that the bairn could scarce breathe, and she shivered as violently as though it were her, Liza Welford, as had been soaked in the water.

Mary Jane ran to her and threw her arms about her, fish guts and all.

"It's all right, love," she told her. "It's all right. The lad's as right as rain, just wet and fearful."

George followed her, carrying the lad who coughed and spluttered, his lips gone rather blue.

"Show me where you're staying," he said. "I'll carry the lad to his home, for I'll have to stop my work to go and change."

Liza just stared up at him, her eyes wide and wild.

"Let's get him back quickly, pet," George touched her arm. "Then he'll not take chill."

Liza seemed to come to then. She nodded, and turned to show the way.

"Come now, lass, let's run."

Mary Jane and I watched them go, reluctantly turning back to our farlanes. It was only then that we saw that Nelly was bent double over the fish troughs, and Jeanie beside her, fishing fresh bandages from her pocket.

"What is it, Nelly?" we cried.

"The puir bairn's got a nasty cut," Jeanie told us. "Och, what a day we're having!"

Nelly straightened herself, but the colour had drained from her face. Blood poured down from the base of her thumb.

"'M all right," she muttered.

Jeanie shook her head. "I dinna call it right. Ye should go hame and get Rachel to clean it properly for ye."

"What's happening here?" the foreman came to ask. "Are you gipping herrings or what?"

He was answered by angry shouts and cries from all the Scotch girls.

"Can ye not see!"

"The lass has cut herself!"

"We'll work when she's taken care of and not before!"

The foreman sighed and Nelly picked up her knife.

"'M all right," she repeated, and snatched up a herring in the tightly bandaged hand and set about gutting it

"I dinna like it," Jeanie muttered, but she went back to her work and we all followed her.

We worked on for the rest of the day and Nelly seemed to recover well, her cheeks soon pink again. It was a long day and we gutted on through the dusk, cheered by the number of barrels we filled and the thought of the money that they'd bring.

Rachel clicked her tongue when she unwrapped Nelly's bandaged hand that night. The cut was deep and nasty, and Nelly flinched as Rachel cleaned it up and smoothed on Mrs Love's ointment.

I don't think any of us were surprised when we heard a hesitant knock on Rachel's door, quite late that night. We didn't leave our beds, we were too tired, but we heard Liza's stumbling miserable voice.

"I'm so sorry, Aunt Rachel. I don't know where else to go."

"Away inside, honey," Rachel told her calmly. "I know well enough what's happened. I've the bed-place made up and ready for you."

It was good to find Liza looking comfortable in her old clothes, knitting furiously by Rachel's fireside when we got back to Henrietta Street after our work the next day. Rachel broke her rule and let us go up to the kitchen in all our muck just to see her for a while, though we'd to promise not to touch anything and not to sit down. Mary Jane was delighted to be back with her friend, though Liza was miserable. She kept going over it all and making herself feel worse and worse.

"How can I go back to Sandwick and tell my mam I'm sacked?" she said. "How could I have let it happen?"

"I don't think it were really your fault," I told her. "I saw the lad. He wouldn't get down. He wouldn't do as he were told."

"I shouldn't have taken him near the harbour," Liza shook her head. "Mam will be so shamed of me, and what will Miss Hindmarch think?"

"That lad had trouble coming to him," said Nelly. "He's maybe learnt summat."

But Liza would only shake her head and sigh. "I've lost more than half the wages I should've earned," she said. "Rachel says that I may stay for a day or two, but then I'll have to go home and face Mam. Do you know what they told me? That I was sacked for bringing him back, wet and smelling of fish! They didn't seem bothered about the danger, just the smell of fish!"

We could not help but smile at that, but Liza was tearful.

"How can Miss Hindmarch take me back as pupil teacher after this?"

"Why don't you write to her?" I said. "You're good at writing, Liza."

"That's a grand idea," said Mary Jane. "Write one of your beautiful letters to Miss Hindmarch and tell her all about it. It can't make things worse."

"Aye," said Liza, thoughtfully. "I'll maybe try."

The catches stayed good for the rest of the week and we worked like beasts. I think it was just the happy thought of the money that kept us going. Nelly gipped as steadily as ever, with her cut hand all bandaged up. It seemed to bother George.

"What made your knife slip, Nelly?" he asked. "You're as grand a gipper as any I've known. Was it the shock of the little lad falling?"

"Aye," said Nelly, blushing. "That were it." Mary Jane grinned saucily at me. We both knew well what it was that had made Nelly go and cut herself, and it wasn't that spoilt little lad.

CHAPTER FIFTEEN

Towards the end of the week, we began to worry about Nelly. When Rachel tended the cut hand each night, she shook her head at the puffy swollen flesh that was revealed.

"The curer's salt won't let it heal," she said. "It eats into the wounds, does that salt. I don't like the look of it, Nelly. You'd do best to let the doctor see it."

"I'm not working like this to spend my money on doctor's bills," said Nelly.

"Why not rest for a day and let Liza go in your place."

"She can't gip," Nelly was stubborn. "None of them can gip like me."

Though she didn't look at all well, we couldn't disagree with that. None of us could gip like Nelly.

We'd another good catch on the Saturday, and I was standing up at the farlanes in the hot midday sun. Nelly worked beside me, but she'd gone very quiet.

"Are you all right, Nelly?" I asked.

Beads of sweat covered her face, and her cheeks had turned red. The look of her frightened me.

"Nelly?" I said. "Are you sick?"

There was no answer, though she carried on gipping.

Then, all at once, the colour drained from her face and she keeled over, head first into the trough of herrings.

"George!" I shrieked, and he was there at once.

"Eh dear, eh dear ... come on lass!" he muttered, pulling Nelly out of the trough. She was still senseless as he heaved her up into his arms. Both of them were covered with fish scales.

He carried her over to the harbour rail. "Give her some air!" he shouted, as people fussed around, curiously. I followed, trembling with the shock of it.

Jeanie dropped her gipping knife and rushed over to us. At last Nelly seemed to revive a little, but then her whole body took to shivering violently. She couldn't seem to stand or even speak, her teeth were chattering so.

"She shouldna be here," Jeanie said, worriedly pressing the back of her hand to Nelly's flushed cheek. "Take her straight back to her lodgings and see she's put to bed."

"Aye," George agreed. "Come on now, pet."

He put his arm round her waist, and set off towards the bridge, half-carrying the girl.

"Can he manage?" I asked Jeanie. "She's a big lass."

"Well, he's a big lad," said Mary Jane. She'd left the packing and come to see what was up. "I shouldn't laugh." She giggled.

"Noo, ye shouldna," Jeanie said, turning cross. "Ye'll noo be laughing if it's the blood poisoning, and I fear it is."

"Oh no," I cried. I didn't like the sound of that and my eyes filled up with tears.

"I dinna ken how ye'll manage withoot her," Jeanie rubbed it in.

We didn't know either, but we set to work again before the foreman noticed that we were short-handed, both of us gipping together and taking turns to do a bit of packing now and then. Jeanie'd been right; we couldn't make half the speed that we'd had with Nelly and I despaired at the sight of the mountain of silver fish in front of me.

"Where's George?" Mary Jane complained angrily. "It's never taking him all this time to find Henrietta Street."

Suddenly tears poured from my eyes, I couldn't stop them, and my hands would not stop shaking as I tried to gip.

SCARBOROUGH SCOTCH FISHER GIRLS AT WORK.

"We can't do it!" I sobbed. "We can't manage without Nelly!"

"Look at ye both," Jeanie sighed, leaving her own farlane and coming to us. "Bairns, both o' ye. Didna I say it. Dinna fret, shove up and make space for me. We canna have ye pickling these fish wi' salt tears."

She set herself to gip our herrings at the speed of lightning.

"Oh thank you, Jeanie," I said, knuckling the tears from my eyes and trying to get on.

She shook her head. "I canna do it for long, lassie."

It seemed ages before George came back, but when he did he brought Liza with him, already wrapped in Nelly's oilskin apron.

"Nelly's awful poorly," she said. "She's in a right state and Rachel's putting her to bed."

"Oh, Liza," I begged. "Will you help us?"

"Course I will," she said. "But I'm not much good at gipping."

"You soon will be," said Mary Jane.

"Bless ye lassie," said Jeanie. "Set her to do the packing, George. Now you two must gip like the wind."

That night we found that Rachel had settled Nelly in the bedplace in her kitchen, where she shivered and shook. Liza's belongings were dumped in our room.

We washed ourselves, then we went up to Rachel's kitchen to see if we could help. It was shocking to find our big strong Nelly weak as a bairn. She'd a rash on her cheeks and she was tearful, not at all herself.

"I'm sorry, lasses," she kept saying. "I'm so sorry."

I'd never heard Nelly apologise to anyone. It made me feel quite sad to hear it. She seemed to go from burning hot one minute to shivering cold the next.

"It's not contagious?" Mary Jane asked, looking alarmed.

Rachel shook her head. "It's as I've feared all along. The poison in that cut has got into her blood, and it's brought on a fever. She must rest and keep warm and quiet, and let me clean that cut each day. It's no good trying to gip with a wound like that."

"So we'll have to finish the season without her?"

"Aye." Rachel was firm about that.

"Well," said Liza cheerfully. "I came as a nursemaid, but it seems I'll go back as a herring girl."

"Do you mind?" I asked her.

"Nay, Dory," she put her arm about me. "It's better far than going home in disgrace."

On Sunday George came round to Henrietta Street and found us in a right taking. Sunday dinner and Sunday service were forgotten while we boiled up broth and herbs and brought bowls of fresh cooling water from the pump. None of it seemed to do any good; Nelly thrashed about in a high fever, shouting out at Rachel and calling for her mam. She stared wildly about her, knowing none of us, two hectic red patches on her cheeks.

Rachel was shaken from her usual calm. "I'm thinking Nelly should have the doctor," she told George. "Though she swore she would not. She keeps crying out for her mam, and I'm wondering if we should send for old Mrs Wright."

"Nelly shall have the doctor whether she likes it or not," said George angrily. "I shall fetch him, and I shall pay him too."

"Will he come visiting on a Sunday?" I wondered, doubtfully.

"I shall make sure that he comes," cried George.

He was back within the hour with the smart doctor who lived up on the West Cliff. The doctor was clearly annoyed to be dragged away from his Sunday dinner, but when he saw the state of Nelly, he spoke kindly and said we'd done right to call him. He sent George running round to the ice-cream man for ice to cool the fever. The doctor said it all depended on us keeping her calm and getting her to rest. He left a special mixture that he said would help.

George was the only one that Nelly would take notice of. While he sat beside her, holding her hand and murmuring gentle words, she'd be still and quiet; but as soon as he moved she'd grow wild again. Poor George sat there all night. In the morning we were relieved to find that she was sleeping peacefully and Rachel was hopeful that the worst was over.

Through the next weeks we worked on at the gipping with Liza in our team. First she did most of the packing, but gradually she began to work at the gipping, and I was very proud to find myself teaching her how to gut a herring. She picked it up quickly and, by the start of October, Liza was as fast as me and Mary Jane.

"Oh, Liza," I said. "We're missing school now, aren't we? It don't matter for me and Mary Jane, but what will Miss Hindmarch do without her pupil teacher? Did you write that letter?"

Liza shrugged her shoulders. "Aye. I wrote it, but I've heard nowt. I'm sure Miss Hindmarch will have had such bad reports of me that I can never face her again." Liza sighed and smiled. "At least my dad has told me that he's proud to see me gipping with the other girls and he says that he's explained it all to Mam."

Each evening George walked back to Henrietta Street with us to see Nelly. He examined the cut hand each day, saying that he'd seen many a nasty cut in his work, but few as bad as that one. Once she was up and gaining strength,

Nelly would walk slowly down to Tate Hill Pier with him, and they'd sit there together, watching the busy harbour.

As the days passed, the work became more patchy and the catches dwindled. There'd be a bad day, and the drifter men would talk of moving down to Grimsby; then they'd have three days of decent fishing and they'd be cheered. All the talk was of the herring movement.

"They're taking off," David Welford told us.

"Aye, for sure," Rachel agreed. "The time has come, they're taking off; they're swimming south."

The Lowestoft men set off for East Anglian waters to chase the black noses, as they called the autumn fish that they caught down there. The Cornishmen stocked up their boats in readiness to follow them.

In the third week of October the dealers went, and the foreman told us that we'd be paid off at the end of the week. The Scotch girls were packing their kist boxes ready to take the train down to Grimsby, though some of them were going as far as Yarmouth and Lowestoft. We'd to top up the last lot of barrels on Saturday, then we were done.

When we got back to Henrietta Street on the Saturday afternoon, Rachel called us up into the kitchen, and said we'd got a visitor. There, sitting by the fireside, sipping tea from Rachel's best china, was our own Miss Hindmarch.

We were so surprised that all we could do was stare at her. She laughed and got up and kissed us all; she didn't seem to mind the smell of fish.

"I'm sorry, so sorry," Liza stammered. "I know I've let you down."

"Oh no," Miss Hindmarch told her. "I think it's quite the other way. I got your letter and I got another letter, too. My friend the photographer wrote to me. He told me how patient you'd been with that awkward little boy, and how dreadfully the child behaved when you visited his studio. How he'd grabbed at all the photographic plates and poked his fingers into the chemical jars. No I think it's me that let you down, Liza. The family were not at all what I'd thought, and the little boy was quite clearly pampered and spoilt. Now will you forgive me, and come back to Bank Top School? I am missing my pupil teacher very much. Indeed, I cannot manage without you."

"Of course I will," Liza smiled happily.

Robbie came running down to Henrietta Street, all excited that he'd got his pay.

"I can't wait to get home and give it to Mam," he told me. "The old fellow says he's taking me back to Sandwick in the *Louie Becket*. He'll take you too, Dory, if you wish. He wants to visit Mam, he insists on it."

"That's right kind of him," I said.

Me and Mary Jane and Liza went to the railway station with Jeanie's gang to see them onto the Yarmouth train.

"Well noo, we're going to miss ye Yorkshire lassies, that's for sure," said Jeanie, hugging us one by one. "Will ye nae come doon for the herringing next year?"

"Aye. We'll come again," we told her.

When we got back to Henrietta Street, we found George and Nelly sitting together on Rachel's step, Nelly's arm comfortably linked through his. Nelly was looking well again, due to Rachel's careful nursing.

"George is off tomorrow," Nelly told us, smiling hugely.

"No need to look so pleased about it," Liza said.

"But then he's coming back," Nelly blushed.

"Oh! Do you mean…?" Mary Jane for once didn't know how to ask.

"Aye," said George. "I'm fixed to work till Christmas, but then I'll be coming back up north. I'll be calling in at Sandwick Bay and I'm hoping that me and Nelly will be wed."

I threw myself at Nelly then, hugging her for all I was worth. She looked surprised and pleased. I truly wanted her to be happy.

"You'll make a right couple, you two will." Mary Jane smiled at them. "Are we to be bridesmaids, then?"

"Can be, if yer like." Nelly looked coy.

It wasn't easy to share out the money that we'd earned. Mary Jane and I agreed that Nelly had a right to claim more than us, as she'd carried us for the first few weeks. But Nelly was full of joy and kindness.

"Fair shares, fair shares," she insisted. "Liza and me shall split the third between us."

The payment that I got seemed a fortune to me, and Mary Jane had enough for a small organ that would fit neatly into her mam's parlour.

So the herring season came quietly to a close, and the Whitby men turned to bait their long lines once more, and braced themselves for the winter gales.

EPILOGUE

On a chilly afternoon in late October, we set out of Whitby harbour in two ploshers, dressed in our best clothes, heading for Sandwick Bay. I was so proud of Robbie, a proper fisherman he looked, wearing the new gansey that I'd just finished knitting in our special Sandwick pattern that we call the waves and herringbone. I went with him in the *Louie Becket*, and Liza, Nelly and Mary Jane followed in the *Elspeth Welford*.

I'd been worried about the journey, for when we'd come to Whitby in July, the choppy water had made me feel thoroughly sick. I'd almost wondered whether to insist on riding home in the carrier's cart, but then I reminded myself that as my father was a fisherman and I was now a herring girl, I should be ashamed. I needn't have worried; the sea was calm, the water like silk, and as we turned towards our bay the sun came out from behind grey clouds and lit up a silver shining pathway before us on the water.

It seemed that half the village was expecting our arrival, for there were all the Welfords down on the staithe to greet us, and Miriam and Alice and Nelly's old mother, Mrs Wright.

"Mam, Mam," Nelly shouted at the top of her voice. "Mam, I'm getting wed."

"Now, young Dory. Don't you go splashing in the water, and getting your good frock all wet," the old lifeboatman told me kindly. He jumped into the water himself and lifted me out.

I ran to Miriam and Alice.

"Lord! I swear you're taller than ever, Lanky Dory," Alice squealed and I hugged her tightly, happy to be called Lanky Dory once again.

"How's our mam?" I begged Miriam.

"Well, you can go and see for yourself." Miriam laughed.

"She's there!" Robbie yelled beside me, pointing to the stone blocks that we used as seats outside the lifeboat house.

"Aye," said Miriam. "She's insisted on walking down the bank to greet you."

"What? She can walk?"

"She can. But it's slow and hard work for her. Go and see."

We both ran over the staithe to our mam, slowing a little as we got close, both of us gone suddenly shy.

"Wei … come home," she said. The words came slow and halting.

"Mam," I cried. "You can speak!"

She smiled and nodded. "Yes. Speak a bit."

She pushed herself up onto her feet, and we both clung tightly to her, laughing and crying all at once.

Then we remembered the really important thing, and we brought out the money that we'd earned.

Mam began to cry, though I think it was happy tears.

"So proud of you … both," she said slowly. "Enough to … see us right through to the spring."

"Now Mam," I said firmly. "I don't want you to fret about money any more. Me and Robbie shall go to work with the herring fleet again next year, and I'm willing to wash and scrub right through the winter, so we'd better start taking in washing again."

Mam shook her head, smiling through her tears.

"Whatever's got into our Dory?" Alice cried out, amazed at my bossiness. "I thought you hated all that soap and water."

"So I did," I grinned at them. "But that's all changed. I'm different now. I'm a herring girl … I can do anything!"

AUTHOR'S NOTE

Although the characters from Sandwick Bay are all fictitious, the main inspiration for the story came from the photographs of Frank Meadow Sutcliffe, the Whitby photographer. The character of the Picture Man is also inspired by Frank Sutcliffe, though it is not in any way intended as an accurate portrayal. Similarly, Sutcliffe's photographs, used to illustrate the book, are not to be confused with the fictional characters I have written about.

I have tried to be as accurate as possible, however, about the character of Mary Linskill, the Victorian Whitby writer. The launching of the lifeboat in *THE FLITHER PICKERS* is based on a real incident that took place in 1901, when the women of Runswick Bay launched the boat with a scratch crew, led by an old coxswain. In the real incident no life was lost and the coxswain needed no persuading. The women were invited to Manchester for a dinner and reception in recognition of their bravery.

In *THE HERRING GIRLS* – the old life-boatman is based on Henry Freeman, sole survivor of the 1861 Whitby lifeboat disaster, though as far as I know his boat the *Louie Becket* was never trapped behind the East Pier as described in the story. Mrs Dryden Smith – Trickey – was a real fisherwoman who lived in Henrietta Street, and was well known for her crafty ways; she appeared in the film, *The Turn of the Tide*. Thomas Langlands was the Whitby lifeboat coxswain in 1902, and for many years after.